A Day For Waving

A Day For Waving

by

Brian E. Turner

Earl of Seacliff Art Workshop
Paekakariki
Aotearoa New Zealand
2004

Cover artwork: 'The Awakening'
Back cover: Portrait of the author

             Both artworks by Grant Lodge

Also by Brian E. Turner: 'The Road Goes On' (ESAW 2003)

Technical Editor: Grant Snow, Precise Print

Printed at Precise Print & Design, Paraparaumu

Published by:

Earl of Seacliff Art Workshop

PO Box 42

Paekakariki

Aotearoa New Zealand

E-mail – pukapuka@paradise.net.nz

ISBN 1-86942-050-0

1

I must say I love flowers. My daughter, Anne, brought me some Iceland poppies when she came to see me today. They weren't flowers bought from a shop, she had picked them from her garden. I looked at them and noticed she hadn't singed the stalks. The flowers won't last if you don't.

"I'm sorry about that Mum," she said.

"Didn't I ever tell you about singeing the stalks?"

"I know. I was in a rush to get here."

This modern world is in such a hurry. It's full of so many labour-saving devices that nobody ever has time to do anything. I gave Anne a box of matches and made her do it right then and there. Or is it there and then?

"We shouldn't be doing this here Mum."

"Go on. Become a daredevil for once."

That is the difference between us. I'm impetuous. I think nothing of lighting matches in a ward where a nurse might come in with a disapproving look. The flowers do make a nice show. After Anne had left I asked for a vase with water. I put them on top of the bedside cabinet. In the morning a petal will have fallen, but that's the way things go.

I keep thinking that she brought me a single red tulip also, although they are out of season. I must have imagined it. A red tulip represents true love. At one time in my life my heart was filled with hatred for my brother concerning a particular incident. But at last enlightenment came and I awoke from the darkness of ignorance to the light of love and forgiveness. This knowledge was like a flower of perfect beauty.

You'll have to forgive me if I get crotchety from time to time. Lack of comfort in the old body, that's the problem.

Anne brought me brandy snaps also. In a brown paper bag what's more. Where did she get a brown paper bag from? You go to the supermarket these days and they put everything in plastic. Except for mushrooms. They give you paper bags for mushrooms in order to enhance the 'natural' image. I suppose straw and chicken manure are natural. But then everything is natural. Plastic and petroleum are also 'natural' because they from nature. Where else would they come from? This bag isn't a mushroom bag. Mushroom bags have the words 'Mushrooms, Finest Quality' printed on them. This is a plain bag. She must have bought it especially from a Brown Paper Bag Shop. You know, the sort of place where you buy incense and candles. No consistency you see. Doesn't have time to singe poppy stalks but goes out of her way to buy brown paper bags because she knows I hate plastic.

Bless her.

Brandy snaps are my favourite sweetmeat, that is apart from the hash cookies my son, Luke, brings. I'm not allowed sweet things here. I hide the brandy snaps under the pillow and eat them when no-one is around. The cookies go into my handbag. God knows what would happen if they found them. They say that sugar and dope are harmful, but how can you do damage to something that is beyond repair? When the doctor saw that Chekov was about to die he ordered champagne. So why shouldn't I have an indulgence?

This Establishment has three Parts. This is the Hospital Part. There is the Retired Part where couples live in Units and the Geriatric Part where those who are Ancient and Decrepit live. They don't call it the Geriatrics Part they call it the Senior Citizens Part. It has to have a pretty name. What's more they spray it with Air Freshener so it will smell sweet. The canister has a picture of a meadow on it and I always associate meadows with cow dung but this freshener spray has a sweet sickly smell. It was obviously manufactured from chemicals. Cow dung has a good healthy smell, bound to clear out the sinuses, and it comes from the intestines of a cow.

You don't have to pretty up age to make it acceptable. Age is as ugly or as beautiful as the person that has it. My children tell me the older I get the more beautiful I become. They really do. I didn't go through the Retired and Geriatric Parts, I came here straight from my home. They had to drag me in. It's a sterile ward, but I have a room to myself and I have some of my things - a photo of my wedding day, an oil painting of the Virgin Mary and other stuff. That's not because I like the Virgin Mary but because it was done by a dear friend, Maisy Brown. I knew her at school. Now we've lost touch. I don't even know if she's living or dead.

Anne and I had a long talk. Many things were resolved. Not big things really, just the little peccadilloes that might mar a friendship, might mar a life.

"I'm not a harridan am I?" I asked.

"No Mum, of course not. Just.."

"Full of beans? Opinionated?"

"I could never be like you."

"Who'd want to be. You know, my dear, I sometimes wish I was a quiet little thing. Then life would be simpler."

"Boring though."

"I was never a bad mother? Was I..."

"When you made me eat rhubarb. I'll never forget it..."

"Rhubarb is good for the bowels."

It's best to wave good-bye to all that. She's a good friend and she'll be here to do all the right things at the last. You know, lay me out, put a lily in my hand and go through all my private possessions. Weep at the funeral too I suppose. I try to tell her I'll be all right, but like most people, she doesn't understand death, she thinks it's some ultimate calamity, not a normal part of existence.

I'm quite confident that I will have a good end you know. How could anything harm me? You might enter into the Tunnel of Mystery in the fairground but there is always an exit. And there is always an explanation for anything that might occur.

People have the idea they are safe from harm because they are a member of some religious order. They hope that if they respect God and perform the proper ritual then death will have no sting. You shouldn't rely on God, you should rely on yourself. Anyway no-one's passionate about religion nowadays, except that I care about mine. I'm a Rationalist.

I thought that would get your attention. Well I'm not a real Rationalist. The fact is I was a Real Rationalist for a time but then my views changed, I became a Liberal Rationalist. A Liberal Rationalist is permitted to be less scathing in his or her attacks on Christianity than a Real Rationalist. The fact is I quite like Jesus. I feel sad that he had to go up on the cross like that. He seemed to be such a really nice person. But then the Christian Church turned him into a Son of God, born of a Virgin, and that has fouled everything up.

I don't like to talk about religion too much although, in a way, it's been the centre of my life. I like to think my views are a little different from the common mould. Trouble is when you talk about it everybody gets upset. People base their whole existence on some piece of dogma without thinking it through. They hold on to this Holy Relic, such as a Piece of Wood From the One and Only True Cross of Saint John, or some such irrelevant icon, in the fond idea that by doing so they will resolve all the wrongness in their lives. And when you try to shake them out of their firm convictions there's bound to be trouble. Why do they cling to these icons?

I was brought up as a Christian but now I reject the faith. Do you want to know why? It is because I cannot accept the superstitious baggage that goes with it. The virgin birth; the inconsistent nativity stories. They say He died to save us from our sins but I can't see much evidence of that. Only womankind can save herself from her sins. Mankind also. Even though those who were closest to me were believers I have to hold to what I know to be true. 'Not prepared to compromise,' do I hear you say? Stubborn and one-eyed more likely.

The staff here are all hovering around waiting for me to pop off. I think they're running a sweep on when it will happen. Doctor Rogers saw me this morning. That young whippersnapper, he told me two years ago that I had six weeks to live. If he'd been any good at his job I'd be away from here by now. Anne said I shouldn't argue with him. I told her when I stop arguing I'll be dead.

I had twelve visitors come to see me yesterday. The staff had to bring in more chairs, but then I've always been short of enough chairs because I love having people near me. When I looked at all those friends sitting around the bed I realised that they were a fair enough symbol of all that I have achieved in my life. I'll tell you about them but you must realise that they are not involved in those things of the past that have been running through my mind at this time, all the people who were the closest to me are gone... all the people I lived my life with... withered blooms in the dust.

Let's talk about the here and now.

Visitors yesterday.

There was Anne and her husband Charles.

There were Anne's two children, Tracy and Glen. .

And Glen's partner, Julie. Julie's blind you know.

Julie and Glen have a wee son, a lovely baby, my great grandson. I was allowed to hold him and he dribbled on my shoulder. They named him Matthew, at my suggestion.

Then there were Milton and Willy who are in my string quartet.

My friend Fred Robottom. President of the Rationalist Society.

And then there was Olive Bush. She's the treasurer of the Horticultural Society.

Last of all my brother's widow Molly and their son William.

Did you count? It was twelve. Of course there are those others, the shadows from the past that are with me always. And I had the strange feeling that Luke was here, though he lives away in the country and did not come this week. Maybe he was thinking about me.

I know I talk too much. You'll have to forgive me for rambling on. If it gets too tedious then you can always close the book.

I don't think I'll go to bed tonight, I'll just sit here in this chair with a blanket over my knees, while the hours pass, and think about the events of my life, grains of sand that trickle through my fingers.

I'll go to sleep when I'm ready. When the light comes.

If you knew me when I was twelve years old you might say: 'How could an innocent, sweet thing like that become what you see here today?' But then how might a smooth brown acorn grow into a knotted and gnarled old oak tree? It is an evolution in which each step follows on from the one before, by gradual increments, inexorably leading to an entirely inevitable outcome.

Not that I really was a 'sweet thing'. I always wanted my own way, even if that led to arguments. Now that I am older I have stopped arguing with the people who are close to me. But I do have an argument with the state of things. There are things wrong with existence and I do not know how to change them. It's too late to do anything about that now.

Childhood was a fairyland. I came 'trailing clouds of glory' into a world of innocence and delight. I now hold that glory in my heart and return to it often in my mind. It was only when the time had passed that I valued what had gone. But we must go from childhood to adulthood. It is a passage that has been ordained for us by some 'other' force that we have no control over, whether we like it or not.

For me the process of growing up commenced on the day that Father delivered his famous sermon about Ugly Jesus.

Sunday mornings were always the same in our household. First I would help Mother prepare the Sunday roast. She peeled the potatoes and the kumara while I shelled the peas or prepared the silverbeet, fresh from the garden. The greens were my responsibility. When she wasn't looking I would eat a raw piece. Much preferable to cooked vegetables. Then it was necessary to Prepare for Church. Sundays were the special days of the week. It seemed as though they were blessed by the Lord, so still and peaceful. That was how I felt until Mother began fussing over my younger brother, Robbie, and myself, with the whole of her nervous intensity, as she made us look our best for church. Of course the whole family were required to attend the service as Father was the Vicar. On this particular day I'd been scrubbed and dressed and curled and pressed to her satisfaction. I asked to go out into the garden while it was Robbie's turn.

"Don't go getting yourself untidy again," she said as I went.

Naturally Robbie was always the last one to be got ready as it was he who was the most likely to get untidy in the shortest possible time. I never got untidy and that is because I value myself. In those days Robbie never did.

The garden was wonderful, Mother's pride and joy, and always so full of flowers, moss, ferns and shady trees. It was spring and the daffodils and snowdrops were out. And with the aroma of beauty I was suddenly transformed, overcome by a feeling of absolute bliss, so strong, so happy. I danced among the flowers and sang. This was what it must be like to be in heaven I thought. But then Mother called out.

"Lucinda, Lucinda, are you behaving yourself out there?" Why did she have to break the spell? And how often did I have to tell her, I'm Lucy, Lucy, not Lucinda. She had every right to christen me Lucinda, and I have every right to be called Lucy if I wish to be.

"I'm here Mother."

"Come inside Lucinda."

"I'm just coming soon Mother."

"Hurry up then, we are leaving for church in a minute."

I came inside and sat on the chair behind her. She was brushing Robbie's hair. You wouldn't think of him as a vicar's son, being so full of mischief as he was, even at nine years old, especially at nine years old.

"Where did you get those nits and knots from Robert?" asked Mother.

"Ouch. You're hurting me."

"Don't be silly. Now hold still. I did give you a comb just last week didn't I? If you used it sometimes you wouldn't have to put up with this. What did you do with it?"

"Ouch. I lost it."

"You lost it? Where did you lose it?"

"I don't know."

"I imagine it was at Jimmy Peabody's."

"No, I was somewhere else."

"What do you mean somewhere else?"

"Jimmy was there. I was combing my hair in front of a mirror and he stole it off me."

Robbie always told such terrible fibs. He was so good at telling them almost everybody believed him. Whenever Robbie told a lie he looked like a little angel. I was always able to tell when Robbie was lying, because of that angelic look, but he was able to fool most other people, even Mother.

"I don't want you playing with Jimmy Peabody."

"Why not Mother?"

"Because I don't. His father doesn't go to church, and he drinks I believe. Lucinda, Lucinda, where are you?"

She hadn't noticed that I had come in.

"I'm just sitting on the chair, Mother," I said.

She looked around and saw me.

"Ah yes. You look nice dear."

"Do I have to go to church today Mother?"

I was thinking about the flowers.

"What do you mean? Of course you are going to church."

"Yes Mother."

"You're not going to be difficult again are you Lucinda?"

"No Mother, I'm not going to be difficult."

I was only occasionally difficult. I tried not to be on Sunday mornings when she had this terrible tendency to act like a martinet.

"Well what's the trouble then? Why don't you want to go to church?"

"It's a lovely day outside. The daffodils and jonquils are blooming."

"I know the daffodils are out. You've had all week to go picking flowers. There's no need to do so this morning. After our Sunday roast you can change your clothes and go outside and play as much as you wish."

"But it's such a happy day."

"It will be just as happy in church. You can learn about Jesus and how He suffered on the Cross to save you. That's the greatest happiness."

"But God is outside in the garden."

"God is also in the church Lucinda. What would your father think if you weren't there?"

"Oh why does my father have to be the Vicar. None of my friends have a father who is a vicar."

"Lucinda!"

I knew there was no way to get out of it. But the fact was I loved going to church and seeing Father in the pulpit and hearing him preach, basking in the respect, even adoration, that he received from the congregation.

"All right then, I'll go to church."

Mother patted Robbie's pockets "Now Robert, you haven't anything in your pockets today have you?"

"No Mother."

"Well if something happens in church like it did last week let us hope for your sake that your father is as lenient as he was then. Frogs in the baptismal font... how did it ever get there... and when Mrs Carthew's new baby was being baptised. I really don't know."

"It escaped."

"How did it get under the cover then?"

"Somebody must have caught it and put it there."

"And who would do that?"

It was not easy for a thirteen year old girl to have a younger brother like Robbie. He was so cunning with his lies. And he expected me to support him. I wasn't going to do that so I told on him.

"He did," I said.

"I did not," said Robbie.

"I know because Susie Peabody told me," I said.

"What do you mean...?" asked Mother.

"I did not, I did not. She's fibbing," replied Robbie.

"I am not fibbing. I can't stand people who tell lies. I just can't abide them," I said.

"Can't abide..." She sighed. "I don't really understand why you children have to be so difficult on Sundays."

The church bell had started ringing which meant that it was time to go. The verger was a punctilious man and could be relied upon to start tolling exactly on time. The sound of the bell calling the congregation to church filled the air with the joy of God. Father came in just then, breezy and affable in his clerical clothes.

"Well, is the family ready for church?"

"Yes Father," said Robbie.

"Robbie, you look just fine."

"Don't call your son Robbie Matthew, his name is Robert."

"Yes Millicent. Oh look here at young Robert, he must have spent a long time brushing his hair this morning."

Father, in fact, usually called Mother, Milly. Sometimes he even called her Milly Molly Mandy.

"Yes Father."

"Well I think we're going to have a brilliant sermon today. I can feel it in me bones."

"But you've not written a sermon this week Matthew. I thought we were to hear one of your old ones?"

"No, I haven't written it down, but I know what I'm going to say. The best sermons are impromptu. I shall enlighten the congregation on the nature of the true Jesus."

"Oh Matthew... Come on now children."

My father would deliver the most interesting sermons. I don't believe the congregation always understood what he was talking about. He was a liberal Christian, just like I'm a Liberal Rationalist, and he asked them to think in new ways. A dangerous practice. I've found, later in life, that people don't always like to think in new ways. It puts a strain on the intellectual and moral capacity. It upsets the safe certainty of experience. I was always excited when I sat in the church on the hard wooden pews and heard him preach the gospel. You could feel the force of his personality, magnetic, charismatic, and yet all the time he spoke from proud conviction. I imagine that if Jesus had come back to life in this century He would have been impressed with my father.

"Today I want to talk to you about Christ. Jesus Christ. The Saviour. The Son of God. Who was this Christ we read so much about? We know He was a man. We know He was a Jew. A Jew? Well He was. His personality illuminates the Gospels, but what did He look like, was He big, was He small, how did He walk, how did He talk? Did He have ingrown toenails? We know nothing of these things, the Gospels do not tell us. I am sure you have all seen illustrations in Gospel stories which describe His life. Pictures of a kindly, meek, beautiful, suffering Saviour.

"But is this picture of truth?

"I was reading in a book the other day which has come down to us from an ancient source. It contained a supposed picture of Jesus and said that He was a runt, that He had a long face and a long nose, and a scraggly beard. In fact He was downright ugly. Of course this source does not have any doctrinal authority. But just suppose, would it matter if He was ugly. You can be sure that Jesus had the features of a Jew, a large nose, broad earlobes, an Adam's apple. I believe also that he was circumscribed.

"And yet when we think of Jesus we do not consider the outward show, we look for the inner light, the light that illuminates the scriptures. The communion with God. He was a man full of God, and full of life, full of laughter. Oh yes, He had a sense of humour, he certainly had a sense of humour. And He talked about the abundance of life and of how we should enjoy it. He gave His life that we might have it, in abundance. It is the message and spirit of Jesus that we should remember, as alive now as it was then. It was a message of love."

After the service we always stood with Father outside the church to greet the congregation as they came out.

"Mrs Robinson-Smythe," said Father. "I trust you enjoyed the sermon."

Mrs Robinson-Smythe was one of those sanctimonious people who are oh so righteous, and for whom any piece of enjoyment is the work of the Devil. She took his hand coldly and went without a word.

"She seems to be a bit off colour today."

"I don't think she enjoyed your sermon, Matthew," said Mother.

"How could she not enjoy it?"

"It may have been a little too, impromptu dear."

Then Old Daniels came up, a humble man.

"Ah Daniels, I trust you enjoyed the sermon. A little, impromptu today."

"Makes you look at things in a different light. Was He really ugly?"

"It has not been ascertained if He was ugly or not."

"Oh well, it doesn't really matter does it. I thought what you said was very, ah, enlightening."

"I'm glad you liked it." Old Daniels shuffled off. There was a light in his eyes. "Well there's someone who appreciates my sermons. Now what about a roast dinner. Nothing like a bit of preaching to whet the appetite."

"Mother I think I'll practice my violin this afternoon," I said as we walked to the manse, which was next door to the church.

"I thought you were going out picking flowers Lucy," said Mother.

"Why would you want to practice your violin Lucinda?" asked Father. He had to make a thing of 'Lucinda' because Mother had lapsed and called me Lucy.

"If Jesus was so ugly then I think He will need comforting with sweet music," I told him.

"I can see I have started a long series of letters to the newspaper. I did not say that Jesus was actually ugly, all I said was that it was possible that He could have been."

"What your father means is that if He was ugly on the outside He was the Son of God on the inside."

"Yes, I thought that was obvious. Come on Robbie."

"Matthew, your son's name is Robert."

"Oh well, so it is."

I suppose it was a childish notion to think that I might be able to make the Ugly Jesus happy by playing the violin. Violins, violas, cellos, that family of stringed instruments are difficult to play because the notes are not found for you, you have to find them by putting your finger on the string in the right position. You have to feel the note, caress it... you have to be able to adjust for the temperature in the room. Mother had given me lessons but somehow I had never been able to find the note. All I could come up with was a lot of scratching. Mother was an excellent performer and had a beautiful tone, mellow but with a touch of astringency. I used to listen to her play in chamber music concerts and could not comprehend how playing could be so perfect.

"It will come one day," she would say. "It will come when you least expect it."

I sat in my room on the bed scraping away when Robbie came in.

"Do I have to listen to that caterwauling?" he wanted to know in his cheeky way.

"You don't have to come in if you don't want to listen."

"I could hear it in the hall."

He sat down on my chair.

"Why don't you go away if you don't like it?"

"I want to know why you told on me."

"I didn't tell."

"You did so."

"It's not Christian to tell lies."

"You got me in trouble."

"I don't want you to go to Hell for telling lies."

"I don't care about Hell."

"You would if you were there." He just shrugged his shoulders. "Did you really put it in?"

"Of course I didn't." He gave his mischievous smile. "She nearly dropped the baby."

"I suppose you thought it was funny."

"You laughed."

"I did not. Why are you always bad?"

"Baddies get all the loot."

"And they get put in jail."

"Someone has to be a baddy. All good adventure books have a villain. When I grow up I'm going to be a robber."

"Don't be silly."

"I don't want you to tell on me."

"Why shouldn't I make sure you are a good boy?"

"I've got a brandy snap. I took it out of the cupboard."

"I'll tell."

"I'll eat it and say you took it."

"Can I have it?"

"Only if you promise not to tell."

"God sees everything you do anyway."

"I don't believe in God."

"It doesn't matter if you don't believe in him, he's still there."

"I don't care. Are you really playing your fiddle for Jesus?"

"Yes."

"That's silly. Have you heard the story about Pat and Mike and Mustard?"

"No, and I don't want to."

He was always trying to embarrass me with schoolboy jokes. Do you remember schoolboy jokes? How inane. It wasn't until his later days that his jokes became humorous.

"I can teach you a trick with twenty-one cards."

"I'm playing the violin."

Robbie went. I picked up the violin and began playing and for the first time ever, the notes were right. I was playing in tune and it was all because of my love for Ugly Jesus.

There are four things that have been the centre of my life. They were all represented on this day.

First there is family.

Second, religion. Such a strong river of philosophy I was subjected to from an early age, and had to resolve.

Third, music, which enlightened my life.

And lastly?

Flowers of course.

2

I thought I heard the César Franck string quartet playing this morning. The only one he ever wrote. Of all the forms of music the string quartet is that which I have the most affinity for. I'm a string quartet person. It is a most congenial combination of instruments and they unite to make a mellifluous harmony of sound. And what is more they are sometimes able to be achieved by musicians of modest abilities, and may be played in chambers of modest dimensions. And that suits me.

But that music, the César Franck, it seemed to come from far away... from over the hills... from the other side of the... I don't know where... How could I have heard it? I have a walkman here but that particular piece is not amongst my tapes. The only other music is piped in, if you call that music, I never turn it on. César Franck? Who was playing it? Ghosts in the mind? Figments of the imagination? Or just a failing memory? It seemed to me that the first violin was very much like Mother's. Fretful, mellow, astringent...

The César Franck is a grossly under-estimated work. It should be played often, even if it is only by figments of the imagination.

Over the hills and far away? Now, that is an orchestral piece by Delius.

Mother taught me all that I ever knew about playing the violin. She had been studying at the Royal Academy of Music in England when she came to New Zealand for a holiday and met Father. That was the end of her serious musical career. There was hardly any opportunity for a professional musician in this country in those days, particularly for the wife of a vicar in a small country town. We New Zealanders were uncultured waifs, far away from the sophistication of Europe. New Zealand audiences once had the bad habit of applauding classical symphonies between the movements. What is more they whistled whilst they applauded. It was only when we stopped doing that that we started to develop Culture. Culture is good, but it sometimes encourages the appearance of stuffed penguins. And, as you know, it's the stuffed variety that get all the fish while the working variety has to make do with leftovers from the table.

Before the Ugly Jesus Sermon Day I never really wanted to study music. Mother trying to impose her will. Me trying to impose my will. (And never the twain shall meet in the arena of agreement.) But after that day I wanted to learn it all. I wanted to find the notes really and truly. I was nice to Mother. I didn't argue with her one bit. I realised that music was to be a part of my life. We were both agreed on following this path of beauty and so we worked together. Conflict disappeared. It was no longer a state of Mother and Daughter, it was a state of friendship. Mother turned out to be a person that I had never known before, intelligent, knowledgeable, gracious. Someone I really liked. But, of course, when it came to household matters, then there was room for disagreement, then we were Mother versus Daughter.

"How will I ever get that tone that you get?" I asked her one day. It was a strong vibrant note. It seemed to be slightly sharp, perhaps slightly dissonant, and yet, you had to say, perfectly in pitch.

"Don't try."

"Why not? It's a beautiful tone."

"You'll have to find your own. It comes from you. If you try to copy someone else then it won't mean a thing."

"How do you do it then?"

"It's not something I ever think about."

"Shall I have a beautiful tone, Mother?"

She smiled. "If you are beautiful."

I looked at myself in the mirror afterwards. No I wasn't pretty, my face was too long. But I wasn't ugly. I looked again and decided that I was beautiful. You don't have to be pretty to be beautiful. Pretty is too even, too regular, it has no character. I thought of Amelia Smith, who was the prettiest girl in class, but an absolute feather-head. She was pretty but without that aspect of asymmetry which makes beauty. I looked at my face and decided that my music would sound like that. And so it has. And as I got older the tone became more mellow. I am silent now of course, but always in silence you will find a note of music.

Mother was a good teacher. She didn't tell me what to do, she taught me to find my own way. That is just so right. You'll never teach anyone anything if you dictate to them what they have to do and don't let them learn for themselves. It's being led to discovery that is the best tutor. If only she had been like that when it came to me making my bed and tidying my room. It was those times in music that we were at peace together. When she picked up the violin and began to play you could see from the look on her face that she was in another world. Engrossed in the music. Over the hills... This is how I like to remember her. This was the real Mother, not the fearful and distressed one that came into being in later years.

Music has been an important part of my life but it was never the centre. The centre of my life has always been the family. I sat all the music exams and obtained all the diplomas that an amateur fiddler might get. Passed *cum laude* also I might say. But when it came to going to University I said - no, I didn't want to devote my life completely to music. You see I knew I was talented, but not prodigiously so. I knew that if I went for a career I would have to play second fiddle to somebody. Is that arrogant of me? No, it wasn't that I was worried about being second best. It was that I would have to put all my energy into the one thing for the rest of my life and, while that life passed me by, the best I would achieve would be mediocrity. I needed to do something that was superlative. When I left school I got a job as an assistant in a hat shop, and sold more hats than had ever been sold before. You see, that was my life skill. Getting on with people, and making friends. Being part of the community. So when someone wanted a hat they would come to me.

It's a strange thing but Life has passed hats by. No-one wears them any more.

I began to teach the fiddle after my husband died. Just for a little extra money. No, I never had a teaching diploma. But if you know people, and you know something about something, you can become a tutor. Students came to me because there were not enough teachers available, and some families could not afford large fees. None of my students ever achieved greatness, not true greatness. One or two went on and eventually got into the Symphony. But it doesn't matter if you're not a bright star in the firmament just as long as you add something to the general benevolence. Culture in our society is created by the impulses and desires of the many, who follow the thoughts of the brilliant few.

Eventually Anne began to develop a talent for fiddle playing so I established a string quartet. I was first violin of course, she was second. Milton and Willy, who came to see me yesterday, are in it. Milton plays the cello and Willy the viola. I call it 'the band' but its proper name is 'The Thorndon Quartet'. We called it that because we met for practice and performance at Thorndon House. You know, the fine old brick building downtown. It was my creation that quartet, just an amateur one but as good as any.

Willy's real name is Wilhemina. She prefers the nickname and who wouldn't. Wilhemina is a name that brings to mind someone yodelling on the Swiss Alps. She has a rare sense of humour. She tells everybody she's Milton's little Willy. Like me she had never wanted to be a professional musician. Even now she's more interested in Greenpeace and the whales. I remember the first time she came to see me. Ten years old. She had a white winter face and a train driver's hat and she looked, oh, so serious when she took the viola from its case, as though it was something sacred. Really she was afraid of it. I never heard such screeching. Still she got the hang of it in the end. She married a good man but fights with him all the time. Too passionate that's the trouble, oh it's a too too passionate cello... They seemed more together yesterday I thought. He held her hand and they smiled at each other. Perhaps they've patched things up, perhaps now that their children have gone at last there's more peace in the house.

Anne's in charge of the band now. She took over first violin when I became too old to play it any more. She's not a bad player but, like me, never likely to achieve more than simple mediocrity. She has other interests and I sometimes get the feeling that she's only doing it to keep me happy. When I wander off that'll probably be the end of it. I don't know why it is, she never tackles anything with intensity. Do you think I've used up all the family energy and left none for anyone else? Oh Anne, Oh Anne, just do something on your own initiative. Do it for me. Do it for the memory of Ugly Jesus.

When I learnt the fiddle I put so much of myself into it. Anne doesn't do that. She is so self contained, detached, doesn't get passionate about things the way I do. I learnt the fiddle for Christ and the family. I wanted to do something to express my appreciation, I wanted to lay at their feet just a small gift, as good as I could make it. Does Anne want to do that for me? Or am I just an old woman, to be humoured?

They've had troubles finding a second violin. There was a young student who showed a lot of promise but he went away to the university in Wellington. Anne had to take on Myra Harbuckle. I keep telling Anne to look out for someone better. You have to be careful about Myra's stringendos, she doesn't know what acceleration means. Still I suppose once you've appointed someone you can't really sack them.

They've been practicing the Borodin, number two. You know it I suppose, full of good tunes like Baubles, Bangles and Beads. A pretty safe thing to do. Borodin would have been a much greater composer if he hadn't had to teach chemistry and wait for his plumbing to be repaired. The trouble was he was that he was too talented, and in too many areas. A highly eminent professor of science at the university. His name even appears in school chemistry textbooks. The only time he ever got to write any music was when he went away on holiday, or was in bed sick. He was friends with all the great Russian composers of the era and they all looked for the day that he would get ill and have time to do his proper work.

Music, that rhythm of sound, so strange and delightful, so much in tune with the rhythm of life, a strong rhythm to soothe the unruly soul, as it goes one two three, one two three, and soon we are dancing to the rhythm of the silent splendour of the heavenly spheres, tuned to the key of the universe, marking time with the rhythm of the eternal.

I wanted to tell about the music, the melody that's strung itself through my life. A thing that never caused conflict nor regret. A thing to heal the wounded spirit, to calm the savage beast. There's music in everything in the world, in the wind and the rain and the thunder, and in the quiet moments when all is still. If you listen carefully you can hear a song in silence, as John Cage can clearly tell us. In silence you find the essence of the world. You have to understand that it is the medium in which sound is contained and that when the sound of the thunder dies away then silence is that which remains and in that silence you can always hear a tiny golden voice.

Where did I hear that music this morning? In the mind? Or was it the angels come to play?

There was a time in my youth that I almost gave up my music. Something vile happened which upset me. I felt anger and hatred towards the perpetrator. At that point in time the hatred would have consumed me, and my music. But I remembered the example of my father and his love of Jesus. There was, in my heart, a small room, where I held forgiveness but never knew it. That saved me. Even so I held on to a misunderstanding for many years, until the truth was finally revealed.

When I was fifteen. The age between that of a girl and a woman. The age when you obtain the advantage of knowledge and lose the joy of innocence. When your body becomes theoretically capable of bearing children, but, to your mind, such a thing is an alien thought. A time when the adults in your world reluctantly begin to accept you as a member of their club. When you step aboard the train that they have been riding with such calm assurance up until then.

My Grandmother Angelique and my Grandfather Ted came out from England on a six week sea voyage and stayed with us for a month when I was fifteen. They had not seen Mother for seventeen years. Now that Grandfather Ted had retired from his job as manager of a foundry they had decided on an extended Overseas Experience, such as we call it nowadays. Grandmother

Angelique was French. She was a most beautiful and attractive person with dark hair, just starting to turn grey, and flashing brown eyes. She told me that she came from Gay Parree and had danced in the Follies. She had a melodious voice and spoke almost perfect English but with a slight French accent. Once, when we were sitting together in my room, she told me about Grandfather Ted. He was a person to call a spade a spade. When she told him about the Follies he said to her that it was not a proper thing for a young woman to do.

"A man with the moral stature who was prepared to state his mind. I fell in love with him right there."

"What's falling in love like Grandma?"

"When it comes you will know. Do you like boys?"

Since I'd began to develop as a woman boys had been an enigma.

"I don't know," I said, not really wanting to discuss the matter.

"You will. Then I will have great grandchildren. But I surely will have great grandchildren anyway, with three daughters."

Mother had two younger sisters, my aunts, living in England, who both were married with children.

"I don't know if I'll ever want to have children," I said. The whole idea seemed just too difficult, too far in the future.

"You will. And when you do make sure you have a son."

"Why Grandma?"

"Ah, your grandfather always wanted a son and I couldn't give him one. All my daughters are married. Surely one of them can be a son for Ted."

"Father will be good enough. He's a vicar too."

She looked at me with a smile.

"Don't tell anyone we talked of this."

She gave me a big hug. I was beginning to like my Grandmother Angelique.

When Grandmother heard about the Kaikoura North Primary School Annual Fancy Dress Ball she decided she would have to make a costume for Robbie.

"We usually hire them," said Mother.

"Oh my dear, this is his last time at the school. No more fancy dress for him is it? Let us make a special one. I can use this sugar bag cloth."

Mother and grandmother had been putting down preserves and had used a whole bag of sugar. It was Robbie's last year at primary school in this small township called Kaikoura North, in the New Zealand countryside where we lived. Next year he would have to travel by bus to the high school, which

I attended, at a slightly larger town four miles away.

"We'll need at least two sugar bags," said Mother. "I kept one from last year. It's in the attic. I assume you have some idea of the costume Mama?"

"A Red Indian I think."

"He'll need feathers for his headdress."

This was solved by Grandfather Ted the following day.

"I saw a turkey bird down on Master Oram's farm. Let me buy that bird and pluck him for our Sunday supper." By supper he meant our midday, after church, roast. "Aye Matthew there'll be a bottle of something good to go with that too by gum, providing you teach the fear of hell-fire to the heathen that day."

"Matthew teaches the love of Christ, Father," said Mother.

"Aye and he does that right well also." Grandfather Ted gave me an enormous wink.

So we had turkey feathers for the Red Indian's headdress. The sugar bags were carefully washed and then dyed dark maroon in the copper. Then there was measuring and cutting and sewing. Before you knew it Robbie had a unique costume for the occasion.

At the Kaikoura North Fancy Dress Ball the children would perform a number of traditional country dances in the first part of the evening. They would practice for weeks at school. I don't remember those dances now. What were they? They were taught to us my Miss Engleton, who took standards one and two. I'm sure she got them out of an obscure treatise on Ancient Airs and Dances that had been handed down to her by some grandparent. Of course at that time they seemed to me to be quite out of fashion. I was going to modern ballroom classes and learning the waltz and the valetta and the foxtrot. The only item I remember clearly was the Grand March which was performed by the whole school as the culmination of the evening. But that wasn't a dance, that was just marching about the floor and criss-crossing in the middle and making an arch with your hands and walking through it. It was done military style to the tune of The Grand Old Duke of York.

The Grand Old Duke of York
he had ten thousand men,
he marched them up to the top of the hill
and he marched them down again.

And when they're up they're up
and when they're down they're down
and when they're only halfway up
they're neither up nor down.

For the evening Mother and I dressed in our best gowns and Father in his ecclesiastical cloth. Robbie looked so pleased in his Red Indian costume. He wanted a tomahawk and when he wasn't given one he did a war dance with loud whoops.

"I'll get shot by a cowboy and bite the dust," he said.

"Why do you want to bite the dust my lad?" asked Grandfather Ted. He had taken quite a shine to Robbie. Thought he would make a good businessman when he grew out of this habit of trying to be bad all the time. Even went to the point of telling Father not to cram Christianity down his throat because it made him worse. Of course Father never crammed anything down anyone's throat.

"Red Indians are baddies. They always bite the dust."

"Ah, some Red Indians are very brave."

"What are you dressed up as, Grandfather Ted?"

"I am dressed up as ballroom dancer my boy. And so is your grandmother here."

Grandfather Ted was resplendent in dinner dress, red bow tie and blue sash. He had a white carnation in his buttonhole. Grandmother Angelique was so elegant in her red ball gown, a marvellous piece of brocade embroidery. They had spent hours preparing themselves, powdering their faces, grooming their hair, painting their fingernails. Yes, even Grandpa Ted painted his fingernails with a clear resin. And he painted a whirl of glue on Grandmother Angelique's cheek and sprinkled pink stardust on it. I saw them there and I thought to myself that that was class, that was how it is done in England where everyone lives in grand houses in the country with servants and horses and rose gardens and afternoon teas.

There was a scene of noise and excitement when we arrived at the Town Hall. All the children were in their costumes, caught up in the joy of the moment. There was Little Bo Peep, the Mounted Policeman, the Pirate, the Faerie Queene, the Cowboy, the Cattle Rustler, The Knight in Shining Armour, the Scary Ghost dressed in a sheet with holes for his eyes, the Dalmatian Dancer in her national costume, the Spider in his web, Superman and the Poor Ragamuffin dressed in rags. Jimmy Peabody was there also. He came as a burglar with a patch over one eye and a bag of loot on his shoulder. Robbie went over to him and said:

"You steal all the jewellery and I'll massacre the pioneers in their covered wagons."

We went to the dressing room to leave our coats. Our Grandparents spent some time perfecting their toilette in front of a most inadequate mirror. I left my violin case there and went up to the stage with the fiddle for I was to assist in providing the music. We were a rather ill-matched piano trio. There was me still finding my way and relying on music sheets. Mother had picked up the cello for the evening. And there was Miss Engleton who went thump thump thump on the upright piano. I knew Mother was competent at the cello but she played with such a noisy vigour and half a semi-tone out of tune. I asked her in an interval what she was doing and she replied that she was trying to get into tune with the piano. Well I suppose a piano tuner would be an unlikely occurrence in a community such as this. But no-one minded the music. All they wanted was a beat. Although our strings were out of tune you might say there was a resonance that, although discordant, gave a special flavour of spontaneity to the performance.

The evening went as usual. For about an hour the children did their dances, culminating with the Grand March. Time for supper. By now the excitement of the start of the evening had run its course The younger children became tired and scratchy as it was past their bed time. They were wrapped in blankets and taken home to their snug beds to dream of dancing around the maypole and lemonade and asparagus rolls.

Now it was time for the adults to dance.

"Where's Robbie?" Mother wanted to know.

"He won't be far away," replied Father.

"I just hope he doesn't go outside and light matches like he did last year."

"I'm sure he's learnt his lesson."

"Will you dance with me Matthew?"

"Of course."

So it was for me to accompany Miss Engleton. But now that the children had gone a dreamy look came over her face and she played with such sweet suppressed passion that my own fiddle seemed to play itself, so fine it was in tune. And I felt for Miss Engleton, now very much an old maid, and the romantic attachments she might have had in her youth, when she had danced the waltz.

Mother and Father danced very badly. Well the fact was that Mother could dance very well, but it was one thing that Father absolutely hated. When they danced it was the only time I saw any friction between them. My grandparents danced very stylishly, as I knew they would. Somehow I thought that they might dance marvellously exceptionally well. The trouble was that whenever they tried to use some floor people kept bumping into them. Mr and Mrs Williams were particularly bad. They were local farmers, the landed gentry. They spoke with such affected English accents and were so, just so so so very much superior to the rest of us, so that when they took to the dance floor the whole of it was entirely devoted to their personal use. Or at least that's what they thought. The song ended at last. Miss Engleton caressed the keys with a final sweet coda.

"I'm sorry my dear, you know I've never got the hang of this dancing." said Father as they came over.

Mother looked at him with daggers but said nothing.

"We will have to give you some lessons, Matthew," said Grandmother.

"He needs more than lessons Mother, he needs feet which know where to go," replied Mother.

"Aye, can't dance mid all that traffic," said Grandfather. "What about you my girl? Would you dance with your old father?"

"I've hardly danced since I've been to New Zealand. No dancing partner. You and mother, show us how it should be done. I'll accompany you on the cello. Solo. You know, like when we used to practice at home."

"Would you like to do an exhibition for us?" asked Father. "I'll have a word with Quigley. Clear the floor for you."

Mr Quigley was the headmaster of Kaikoura North Primary School and had been acting as Master of Ceremonies. Father spoke to him and he went to the stage and called for silence.

"Ladies and Gentlemen. As some of you may know Mr and Mrs Poynting are currently visiting our fair shores from the Old Country." Polite applause. "The Old Country, that some of us still refer to as Home." Mr Quigley was always liable to prolong any speech he made with such boring irrelevancies. "Indeed they have come to visit their daughter, the wife of our dear Vicar, and her family." Polite applause for the wife of the dear Vicar and her family. "I have been advised that Mr and Mrs Poynting are experts in the discipline of ballroom dancing. I have here a list of prizes they have won in England but the list is so long I hesitate to read them out lest proceedings be delayed unduly." Ironic cheer from anonymous wag in the back. "Mr and

Mrs Poynting have kindly consented to provide us with an exhibition of ballroom dancing in the modern style." Applause. "Ladies and Gentlemen, I give you a twilight waltz."

Mother played a chord on the cello. A dark, vibrant, mysterious chord. A chord with some authority. My Grandparents entered the dance floor on this cue and stood motionless in their silhouette. He so tall and grave. She, resting in his arms like a swan, with her head back and her fingers splayed in a pattern on his shoulder. So elegant. And then Mother played the melody with such romantic passion. "After the Ball is Over". And the two began to dance with such grace and perfection of style, with such finely realised mannerisms that to me the performance was a sublime perfection of art. I could see them dancing in heaven among the clouds to an audience of angels. I could see that even God would applaud.

At the end everyone clapped loudly. Mr Quigley took the stage. "I'm sure everyone will show their appreciation for that marvellous exhibition in the usual way." Applause. "And now gentlemen, take your partners for a foxtrot..." And the farmers and their wives shuffled around the ballroom again in a noisy imitation of combine harvesters.

Angelique leant her head on Ted's shoulder.

"You'll have to learn how to dance my son," said Grandfather Ted to Father. "It's the only thing I can do that keeps her happy. We will give him some lessons, won't we dear?"

It was the first time he called Father son. He did take the lessons and next year he and Mother danced a passable waltz at the Kaikoura North Annual Fancy Dress Ball.

Later Father rang the manse. Robbie was there and was going to bed.

"Leave him," said Father. "He's old enough not to need us there."

"I wouldn't like anything to happen," said Mother.

"Don't be silly, he'll be perfectly all right."

Mother reclined in Father's arms as they attempted to dance, but she kept looking over her shoulder. I could see she would worry. I told them I was tired and wanted to go home. I took my fiddle down to the dressing room. When I opened the case I couldn't believe it. Neatly, laid in the centre of the velvet, was a human turd. I just couldn't believe it. What a vile foul thing to do. I took the case to the toilet, picked up the turd in toilet paper and flushed it down. Fortunately the turd was hard and made little mess. I felt violated. I could not put my fiddle back in that case, not until it had been fully sanctified. Who would do such a thing?

Of course, it had to be Robbie. For that he would never be forgiven. Even after he was dead and burning in hell he would never be forgiven.

I crept back to the manse. Robbie was in the kitchen in his pyjamas with a biscuit and a glass of milk. I said nothing to him. I was not going to give him any satisfaction over this matter. No satisfaction of knowing how much he had hurt me.

Over the weeks I thoroughly cleansed the violin case with eau de cologne and aired it by the window. Even today I wince when I place a violin in its case.

3

I've been thinking about the people who came to see me yesterday. There was Anne, of course, and her husband Charles. As a person Charles hasn't got many major faults. On the other hand he doesn't have many prominent talents. I find him a bit wet at times, and he works in a bank. I always had a prejudice against bank clerks. Anyway she likes him. She's always telling me what good mates they are, as though she has to reassure herself. But being a good mate is not... being in love... Their marriage is not perfection. It's just something they got into by accident and now they're in it they don't know what to do to get out of it. And if they did get out of it they still wouldn't know what to do with themselves anyway. They're each a part of the other's furniture. Well at least they're friends. I wouldn't be very happy if she was alone and sad.

Once I thought that in the end everything might be perfect, that everyone would find true and eternal love and settle down and live happily ever after. But that's the contrived ending for fairy stories and popular novels of love and romance. It doesn't happen in real life. Real life just goes on without any rhyme or reason. Maybe we are all waiting for Godot, who never comes... I was in love, but it was not a fairy story and it did not end in perfection. It ended when my love, who was my husband, died.

I imagine if everything were perfect there'd be nothing to do and we'd all get terribly bored. Try and think of Heaven where all was absolutely pure alabaster and marble. Once you learned to play the harp and sing in the choir that would be the end of it. You'd be so bored you might want to go down to the other place for a little variety. Fact is you are never so happy as when you're striving to overcome obstacles, so what's the point of a place where everything has been achieved and there is nothing more to be done? I'm sure that an eternity of pure happiness would drive anyone around the twist.

Charles is a Roman Catholic, that's the problem. Our family have always been Protestants. It doesn't worry me that he's a Catholic. The trouble is he's not at all passionate about it. Anne complains to me that I don't like Charles. Well, it's not that I hate him. I mean there's nothing outright odious about his character, it's just that he doesn't seem to be able to make me aware of his presence. I do make an effort, but when you tap on the bell and there's no sound what are you to do?

These visitors that came to see me yesterday, they are all part of the here and now. They are the result of my life story, but they are not the centre of it. All those who were with me once upon a time are all gone. They are the ghosts that haunt me, and beckon me to join them.

I've been dreaming about the old days with roast dinners and languid sunny Sunday afternoons. Lamb with potatoes and peas and mint sauce, or sometimes a roast of beef with Yorkshire duff. Peas out of the garden too. The peas you get today come in packets and they are soft and squashy when you cook them. They dye them you know. The peas that come straight from the garden, they aren't so green but they are real peas.

Your head is in a different space when you are a child. Thoughts are quite different. In a way it's a bit like being stoned. You think it's unusual for a great-grandmother to be into drugs? Well, I suppose not many are, but you see, I am the sort of person that enquires into the nature of things so I will try anything. It was about ten years ago my son, Luke, told me he smoked marijuana cigarettes so I said I wanted to try one. We shared it and for a magic moment I entered into fantastical world where the senses were heightened. And my thoughts and feelings returned to the world of my childhood. I felt like a child, and I thought like a child.

So a substance can change the way you think, but can it change the being you are? Does that mean that your thoughts are just a cocktail of various chemicals? Some people would say so. At puberty our wit becomes sharper and our innocent 'intimations of immortality' fade. It was as though through all my childhood I was under the influence of a drug that heightened awareness of sensation. And when I become adult something strange happened to blunten feelings and sharpen the intellect.

Now the youthful ambition and anguish have dissolved and the aged body approaches its final dissolution, we are sent to a second childhood, but a childhood where the world is old, tawdry, familiar...

So the question is; are we chemicals or spirit, or are we a bit of each? If God gives us a soul where does it come from? And when you die does it go up to heaven or down to hell for all of eternity? Or was it always there? Or is it something other that you? Or is it you?

You see I am a Rationalist and I approach these questions in a rational manner. If your thoughts change as the result of chemicals then your thoughts must be made up of chemicals. That is a logical conclusion. But it doesn't mean to say that chemicals are the only aspect of your thoughts. Spiritual matters could also make up your thoughts. I mean if we are a mixture of matter and soul then our thoughts might also be a mixture of matter and soul.

"Yes." Cain looked uncomfortable. "Look Vicar, you know I'm an Agnostic..."

"Yes, we do know you are an Agnostic Cain."

"I should be getting back..."

"We don't mind talking to Agnostics. Jesus Christ spent most of his life in communion with criminals and prostitutes, not to mention members of the Inland Revenue Service. He said those were the sort of people that needed salvation – more so than the sanctified. We are not like the Scribes and the Pharisees you know, we admit all peoples into our presence. I don't care if you are an Agnostic, or even a Roman Catholic, Cain, you can be a friend if you like."

"Yes Vicar."

"If you don't talk to me about your religion then I won't talk to you about mine."

"Yes Vicar."

"And call me Matthew."

"Yes, Matthew."

Father burped and looked at Mother. "You were right about that ginger beer, dear."

Cain looked at me, and then back to Father. "Ah Vicar, Mr Tunnicliffe..." Father studiously looked at the sky. "Matthew..."

"Yes Cain?"

"There's a standing pool just down past the bend..."

"A standing pool?" asked Mother.

"Still water. It's caused by a meander which has since moved away."

"Ah yes, a meander," said father

"We're doing a study of river-life at school. I thought Lucy might like to see it."

"You should ask her, not me. Is there a sandwich left?"

"You ate the last one Matthew," said Mother.

"Did I really?"

"There are flowers growing on the river bank," I said.

"What kind of flowers?" Mother wanted to know.

"Wild daisies."

"Wild ones... not those with all that yellow pollen?"

"I don't think there's any pollen Mother."

"Well as long as they're... Don't be too long dear, we'll want to get home before dinner. And don't get into stagnant water. It can be infected you know."

Cain and I walked off down to the riverbank. Then I realised that I had forgotten my hat. One cannot be seen walking with a man unchaperoned without one's hat, so I went back to get it. They had their backs to me and I stopped and stood behind a tree because I heard Mother mention our names.

"Ah, it's a sleepy day. I told him, I told him didn't I?" Father put his arm around her and she leant against his shoulder. They looked so peaceful, so much in love.

"I think they care about each other."

"Who?"

"Lucy and Cain."

"Do you think so?"

"Yes."

"You mean in love?"

"Perhaps."

"He's a fine young man."

"He's an Agnostic Matthew."

"It's only what his father preaches. He's a fine young man."

"And you'd let her marry him?"

"Of course. Maybe we could convert him. I imagine if our Lucinda wanted to do something you wouldn't be able to argue her out of it."

"Too headstrong that girl."

"Not really headstrong. Just sure of herself."

Of course I was never headstrong. Mother had such strange ideas about me at times. And were my feelings towards Cain so apparent? I was greatly embarrassed. These feelings I had were private. I never told anyone. How could they possibly know? They were feelings I didn't even fully understand myself.

"Matthew?"

"Yes dear?"

"There's something I wanted to ask you."

"What was that?"

"I am a good wife to you aren't I?"

"Now that's a silly question to ask."

"Yes, I suppose it is. I can be bossy..."

"A little bit. Occasionally."

"And I make a fuss if things aren't tidy."

"You have been known to."

"On days like this I feel so happy, with you and the children, and our life. It seems like perfection."

"It's a good Christian life. It's what it should be."

"I know. But sometimes..."

"Yes."

"Sometimes I feel uneasy."

"Uneasy?"

"The world isn't perfect is it. There are terrible things in it. They never seem to go away. Even though our lives are good and pure. Even though we do our utmost to prevent them."

"There are bad things...."

"But why are there? Why can't God just make everything perfect?"

"That's not for us to..."

"Why does there have to be evil? I read in the papers about the political situation in Europe... there's this depression and people out of work. Some of the church mothers don't even have milk for their babies. I don't know where it will end Matthew, I don't know where it will end."

"Don't worry my darling, don't worry, nothing will ever come to bring you harm."

"Nothing bad will come? Nothing evil will come to destroy everything? Will it?"

"No, nothing bad will come."

"And God will care for us?"

"Yes, God will care."

I didn't get the hat after all. Still I didn't have to be privy to private conversations to know what was going on within a family. Even on a cloudless day there are shadows. Mother hoped that life would be eternal sunshine. You can see how anxiety can be created. One lives a model life, seeks goodness, perfection, yet the seeds of sin, distress creep in... and then there is conflict...

The simple law of life is that perfection cannot be attained. Everything naturally inclines towards the mean, half way between the absolute of Heaven and the absolute of Hell. It is only in that position of mediocrity between the two extremes that peace and happiness can be found. For that is the state where life is in balance.

Cain took me to the pool of stagnant water that he had found. Once the river had run there but then its course had changed and it had left a small pond behind. The pond was covered with green weed and looked quite noisome. There were clumps of yellow daisies on the bank beside and I started to pick them.

"Do you like flowers?" asked Cain

"I'll take them to heaven with me when I die." That is true. If I'm ever invited into heaven I shall take baskets and baskets of bouquets with me. Not only that I'll ask His Lordship if I can have the job of chief gardener.

At this point Robbie came by.'"You two haven't seen Jimmy have you?"

"I thought I saw him back by the old scout hut," replied Cain.

"No, he's not there."

"What are you two up to anyway?" I had to ask him about his mischief.

"We're going to catch some trout."

"I thought you were going eeling."

"No. You didn't tell them I was going eeling did you?"

"Mother said you were going eeling."

"I bet you told her that. What does she know? We're going to catch trout."

"Well I expect to see one on the dinner table tonight."

"We're going to use a net, but I can catch you a big slimy eel if you want one."

"Nets are illegal for catching trout."

"I shouldn't have told you, you're just a tell-tale."

"If I find out what you've been up to I will..."

"I don't care what you say. I'll do what I want to do. I'm going." Robbie went.

"I just wonder what mischief they're getting up to." That picture of the turd in the violin case would not leave me. It was terrible having a brother who would do a thing like that.

"They're probably going down to the old scout hut to smoke cigarettes and swap dirty stories." Cain was just naive. He'd never had a brother.

"That's the least they're likely to do."

"It's what I used to do when I was his age." Cain paused and looked at me, wondering, I think, whether he was familiar enough with me at this stage to ask a personal question. You see how relationships might start. When you first meet you act in a very formal manner and then you gradually become less formal, more familiar. Eventually you will step across boundaries, and each time you make a step you make a decision to either become closer or to withdraw.

"You don't get on with Robbie do you?"

"What makes you say that?"

"It just seems... He seems a decent chap. A bit high spirited..."

"You don't know him like I do."

"No. I suppose I don't."

"He's bad to the core." I think I was trying to shock Cain at this stage. Try him out. See if he wanted to be a part of this family.

"Well not really."

"He never does anything good."

"Is he supposed to?"

"He's a Christian isn't he? Christians are supposed to be good."

"I thought there was a bit more to Christianity than that."

"What do you know about it, you're an atheist."

"I'm an agnostic really."

"Agnostic then." I looked at Cain. We might or might not be in love, but we had at least reached the status of being friends, able to confide in each other. "Well it's time he grew out of it. Kid brothers are an anathema don't you think?"

"I don't know."

"Why not Mister Agnostic?"

"Because I never had a kid brother, and I don't know what anathema means."

"Something cursed by God."

"Cursed by God? The Old Testament God I assume."

"Oh? Why?"

"The Christian God didn't curse. He was the God of love. The Father."

"So it's a Mister Theologian too is it?" It annoyed me so much that an agnostic seemed to know more about religion than I did.

"Why not?" I did not know what to say to that. He took a notebook and pencil from his pocket and sat down beside the pool. "What do you think?"

"It's just a pool of stagnant water, covered with green slime."

"That's not slime, it's duckweed. See, small petals. It serves to oxygenate the water."

"Is this what we are supposed to be doing our study about?"

"This and the whole river."

"I don't see the point of investigating this."

"You have to look under the surface. Pools like this are the breeding ground for half the insect life on the whole river catchment." He moved the duckweed aside with a twig. The water was murky and there were ugly wriggling things in it. They were like maggots with twin tails. "See, dragonfly larvae."

I didn't know actually what they were but I had to say something. "More like sandfly larvae."

"No. Dragonfly. See there's one."

There was a dragon-fly hovering over the pool. "Do they sting?"

"Yes. Be careful. Just think, in one day they are born, mate, lay their eggs and die."

"That's not dragonflies, that's mayflies you're thinking of."

"No, dragonflies. Real dragons guard their treasure under magic mountains, but if it gets stolen they have to fly around to find it. That's when they become dragonflies."

"Don't be silly." I looked at the dragonfly hovering over the water in the lazy summer afternoon, a stick with gossamer wings, thinking of its treasure. "Dragonflies live longer than mayflies, read your textbook properly."

"It might be." He looked at me with concern, then asked another question. A further step towards familiarity. "Are you all right?"

"It's all perfect isn't it, a grassy river bank, flowers, a cloudless sky, I should be ecstatically happy."

"Aren't you?"

I had to think before I answered that. Was he allowed into my private world of thoughts and emotions? "That's my business."

"I suppose."

"Is it possible to be ecstatically happy when you're nineteen?"

"But I'm nineteen and I am ecstatically happy."

"Don't be stupid, you are not."

"No. I'm not ecstatically happy. But I am happy."

"Happy?"

"Content."

I didn't want to talk about it. There were times when I was enveloped by such a feeling of melancholy. A feeling that there was no reason for my existence. That I would never be able to enter into that strange world of adulthood that loomed before me. I had to change the subject.

"I haven't started my project yet, you can help me if you like."

Cain looked at me. He decided to press forward. "I've got a friend who's ecstatically happy."

"I don't want to talk about it."

"His name's Bozo. Do you want to talk to him?"

I put down the flowers and walked over to the bank and sat down. "I don't want to talk to anyone."

"Bozo, Bozo. Chee chee chee chee." He bounded around like a monkey scratching under his armpits, jumping up and down.

How childish. How stupid. "Bozo's a dog's name."

"Bozo not a dog. Bozo a simian. Chee chee chee chee."

"Why don't you stop being so silly" He was really starting to annoy me. Had I come in contact with a madman? It really was too silly.

"Bozo silly, Bozo got simian brain, Bozo got a sillian brain. Chee chee chee chee. Bozo do somersault."

He started doing somersaults but he was very awkward and didn't look where he was going. I had to grasp him by the arm to stop him from going into the pool. "Watch out, you'll go in the water."

"Bozo not like water." He looked at me, right into my eyes, somehow into my soul. I let go his arm.

"You are silly." I started to laugh.

"Bozo silly, Bozo silly, Bozo silly simian."

Suddenly it was so funny, so ridiculous I couldn't stop laughing. I wanted to hold him, hug him close to me. I went to him and gave him a peck on the cheek and then ran back to the daisies.

"You are sweet," I said.

He just stood there, no longer a monkey and looked at me quite seriously. "I love you Lucy."

"Yes." I didn't know what to say.

"Do you love me?"

"My parents think I do."

"What about you?"

What exactly did I feel at that stage? It was something I could not explain or understand.

"It could just be infatuation Cain."

"Infatuation?"

"It could be that I'm just so dissatisfied because someone of my age needs love. How do I know for certain that you are the right one?"

"I don't know. That's something you have to find out." He sat down on the grass and picked up my bunch of daisies. "I want permission to start courting then."

"Permission?"

"If I can convince your father..."

"Don't worry about Father. It's Mother you will have to convince."

"Or you..."

He held out the flowers. I hesitated. If I took this gift from Cain then he would no longer be a stranger, we would have to always be friends. Then I knew that was what I wanted. I took the flowers.

"One would hope so," I said.

4

I was quite pure at that time you understand. Unstained by carnal contact. But there was a wild animal lurking within which had been tamed by convention. The unrequited lust consumed itself, became foul and tainted by canker. It was a furled, voluptuous, bud, that urged to break out, to burst into flower. I loved Cain on that day. I wanted to drag him into the long grass, to release the stale retention and become a woman, someone who knew the mysteries of life, someone who looked at the world with a secret smile of private understanding. Instead I followed the dictates of society. My parents expected that. Christian morals expected that. To remain a virgin until I was married. To own myself completely without ever letting the corrupt thrust of the world into my chaste kingdom.

Growth is difficult, painful, the husk of the hard nut must split before the germen in the kernel shoots forth.

When I think of growth I think of plants. That reminds me of Olive Bush who was one of my visitors the other day. She's the treasurer of the Horticultural Society. You might think that her parents were cruel to call her Olive, but the fact is she fell in love with a man called Fred Bush and married him. Her maiden name was Gard'ner. Olive has got green thumbs, and green toes and green just about everything else. She's so good for a garden. To look at her you would almost believe that you could see corn sprouting out of her ears. I used to be treasurer of the Society before she took over. I taught her about the books. It was Mother that taught me how to make things grow but it was Olive that taught me about the secret words that the plants understood. She also taught me how to invoke the gods of earth and air and about the subtle influences of the stars and the moon and the cycle of the universe. The cosmic influence on growing things is very profound. Esoteric knowledge. I am not going to reveal that here. It is available and if you are worthy you will find it.

Olive taught me about modern agriculture also. How fertilisers fill plants with quick bland growth so that all they give is bulk and little goodness. About how insecticides leach into the earth and so become incorporated into the flesh of the plants we eat. They kill tiny animals quickly and large animals slowly. Did you ever wonder why cancer is on the increase? It plots along with the use of poisons in agriculture. The only tests of protection that research scientists do are to ensure that insecticides do not kill large animals quickly. But who knows what slow effects there might be?

Thought I'd give Olive's views a bit of a plug.

Yes, I remember back to the time when I was a growing, developing being, passing from one stage of growth to the next. Not so now. There comes eventually a time in your life when you cease to grow and all that you are left with is a slow decline.

Growth, yes growth. I have considered quite carefully this matter of generation. It is a thing of some moment. We take it for granted because it is so familiar but there is more here than meets the mundane eye...

We know that things grow. Scientists have observed the process and described the steps in detail. But although we understand the method of growth we do not understand the agency behind it. I might say to people that I grow radishes or carrots or Mexican marigolds. But I don't actually cause anything to grow. All I do is plant a seed in the earth and provide water, manure and a little cultivation. There is some power, force, agent, law of the universe, whatever you might call it, quite independent of myself, that converts the seed into a plant. There is another determinacy which is at work in this matter. We call it Nature and leave it at that. But what is Nature? In ancient times it would have been personified in the form of a fertility goddess. It would have to be female of course, because females give birth. Someone like Olive with flowers in her hair and barley coming out of her ears. She would be given a name and statues would have been carved and she would be worshipped in the springtime with pagan rites. But that does not help in the understanding, all it does is give it a symbol. Nowadays we also apply a symbol, in the form of a chemical analysis in a laboratory. We describe the structure of the DNA and say that defines life. We must do it like that because we no longer give currency to primitive pagan goddesses and Bacchic rites. But neither Bacchic rites or laboratory analysis tells me what it really is. Can anyone explain to me what it is that makes Nature work? It's a complete mystery you see.

It's the same with your life, you live it but you know nothing about why you are here or what you are doing, or what made it. You just arrive in it, a smelly little bundle of needs, desires, affections. The adults have been riding the train for some time and by this time have found out what is expected of them, and after a while you get to learn that you are expected to do certain things, and not do other things, and that's how you live a life. You learn to play the game as it has been played, with variations, for thousands of years. But what is this game? Is it anything more than a series of arbitrary actions, or is it some sort of charade designed to amuse the gods in Valhalla. No-one comes down from Heaven to tell you what it's all about; and no-one comes along with a ticket for your departure either, or any explanation as to why you have to go, or whither thou goest. You see we are in control of nothing.

Now forget about growing things. We come to the topic of religious studies. I relate these two topics of growth and studies in my mind because the studies usually took place in the gazebo in the garden. How did they come about? Yes, it was at the instigation of Cain's father when I became engaged to Cain.

Of course once Cain and I had started courting, and our feelings for each other had become established, Montague was invited to visit the manse for afternoon tea. He came dressed in loud ginger checked plus-fours and a monocle. Also he wore a dark blue shirt and a white tie. But the eccentric clothes were only for exterior inspection. Beneath that he was a serious person. An intellectual but always a jovial and charming companion.

"How can an atheist be such a nice man?" said Mother when he had left.

Father had smiled; "How could Rasputin be such an evil one?"

After this Montague visited us often and on occasions we went to his house to savour 'bachelor cooking'. Montague, in his astute way, never mentioned Religion in Mother's presence, however I believe he had long discussions with Father in private.

Cain and I were in the garden one day.

"Montague wants you to become an atheist," said Cain.

"What do you mean? He wants me to become an atheist?" I was most indignant.

"Well I exaggerate I suppose."

"I suppose you do."

"Well, seeing as I attend church and listen to Matthew's sermons he feels it's only right that he lecture you and me on Rationalism."

"You and I." I was going through a pedantic 'correction-of minor-errors-in- grammar' phase. "Mother won't like that. She wants you to become a good Christian."

"You never know, she may achieve her wish. Montague spoke to Matthew and it was agreed."

"I'm old enough to know if I want to take lectures on any subject or not."

"Don't argue darling."

"I'll argue if I want to."

He sighed. "It's arranged."

"I'll take one lecture and if I think it's acceptable I might consider taking more. I hope you understand I will not be taken for granted."

I flounced off. But, in fact, I did find the lesson most interesting and decided to take more.

I had accepted Christian dogma with simple innocence until I was over twenty years old. The fact is I'd never really thought about it deeply. It was part of my social environment, to be accepted and relied upon. Also I loved and respected Father. Such a good man, intelligent, charismatic. So sure in his beliefs that nobody could ever possibly doubt them.

Montague and Cain started coming to church and would join us for the Sunday roast. Montague would bring one of his own gastronomic creations for dessert. After the meal he and Cain and I would go to the summerhouse for instruction. I remember the first time Mother said in her nervous way: "You will be all right dear?" Of course I would be all right, but it was then that the seeds of doubt were sown. Poor mother. To think that she believed that if someone lost their Christian faith the world would crumble and dissolve.

Montague took his Rationalism more seriously than Father took religion. Cain was somewhat embarrassed. He kept looking at me with apology in his eyes. Apology for having put me in a position where this pagan polemic was to be inflicted. Apology for the views of his father. Yet I was beginning to find these ideas quite… quite amenable. Cain, on the other hand, had been spending too much time with Father, always pestering him about certain theological questions.

I remember sitting in the summerhouse with Montague and Cain one particular Sunday afternoon. (On these occasions Montague would always wear a dark suit, a white shirt and a black tie. Cain told me that it was because his mother had died on a Sunday.) We had been discussing the improbability of the nativity myths.

"You mean there's no *Away in a Manger*?" I asked.

"I'm afraid not," replied Montague.

Then Cain had to butt in. "This picture you have of animals in a barn is totally false Lucy. You see it says the babe was laid in a manger, which is a food trough for animals. There's nothing in the Bible to say it was a room full of animals, but somehow people think that is what a manger is. I imagine

Joseph spent all his time at the tavern and never got round to making a proper crib."

"We are not going that far my boy," said Montague.

There was a tension between father and son. Cain wanting to break away from the polemical apron strings and wasn't yet sure how to do it.

"Well that's the story that Matthew told me."

"How Matthew can be an Ordained Minister of Religion and have such views is quite beyond me. Joseph a drunk, Mary a whore and Jesus a bastard. There's little basis for such beliefs. If I espoused them, being a Rationalist, I'd be castigated. And when I point out to him the fallacies of the Bible he just smiles and says 'so what?'."

"Surely Joseph wouldn't have taken his carpenter's tools all the way to Bethlehem." I said.

"There never was a trip to Bethlehem," replied Montague.

"Matthew says the story of the manger was probably the distant memory of a real event, back in Nazareth," said Cain.

"We'll deal in facts not suppositions." Montague opened the Bible at a marked place. "John, Chapter seven, verses forty to forty-five. 'Many *of the people therefore, when they heard this saying, said, Of a truth this is the Prophet. Others said, This is the Christ. But some said, Shall Christ come out of Galilee? Hath not the Scripture said, That Christ cometh of the seed of David, and out of the town of Bethlehem, where David was? So there was division among the people because of him. And some of them would have taken him; but no man laid hands on him.*' Now what do you make of that?"

I looked at Cain. Apparently it was intended that I answer this question. "It says that the crowd didn't think Jesus was the Messiah because he was not born in Bethlehem and was not descended from David."

"And what does that mean?"

"That Christ was not the Saviour?" I had decided to be obtuse. I just hated to be asked questions in this patronising manner. Cain came to the rescue.

"Because it had been prophesied in the Old Testament that a Messiah would be born in Bethlehem and descended from David."

"Ah, there's the nub. Inconsistency in the Biblical records. Do you see? Do you see Lucy?"

"What does it matter where he was born if he was still Jesus?" This exposure to rational thought had been having an effect on me, breaking down my long held misconceptions, but I didn't wish to admit to that openly.

"What we are pointing out here is that John says that Jesus was not born in Bethlehem but that Luke says he was."

"It doesn't really matter where he was born. He would still have been the same person."

"I know that Lucy, I know that. What I'm telling you is that there is an inconsistency in the Biblical reports."

"So Luke invented a story to make the prophecy come true?"

"Precisely." Montague was very pleased that I had seen this.

"And what about being descended from David? That was another Old Testament prophecy."

"Exactly. Matthew and Luke both have genealogies that link David to Joseph. Both different..."

Cain broke in. "Matthew tells me that many theologians don't believe the nativity stories."

"Matthew should know better than that if he's an advocate of Jesus Christ," I said.

"I'm just repeating what he said." Cain turned to me. "Look we're not trying to tear down your beliefs..."

"If I've been taught something it doesn't mean to say I have to believe it."

"Yes, well that's all right then. I think we've done enough for one day." Montague closed the Bible. "I have things to do at home. I'll tell Matthew and Millicent that we've finished. Are you coming up to the manse?"

"They said they'd come here with afternoon tea," said Cain.

"Of course."

He left.

"I find this very interesting," I said.

"Well I've had it thrust down my throat all my life."

"But it is true. The gospel authors made things up to agree with prophecy."

"I'm not concerned about the literal truth of the gospels, I'm concerned about the underlying truth..."

"What underlying truth?"

"Have you never spoken to your father?"

"Of course I've spoken to my father, I speak to him every day."

"I mean about Christianity."

"No, I get lectures about Christianity from Mother."

"I've had long discussions with Matthew. There are no doubts that there are inconsistencies in the New Testament reports of Jesus. Matthew accepts that. If you insist that God is infallible then Christian beliefs are a nonsense, but if you throw away the myth and accept Christ for what he is you..."

"You spend too much time talking to Matthew."

Father and Cain had become very close friends and spent a lot of time together. I had no idea what they talked about when they were alone. When they were in company the only topics of conversation were sports or current affairs, which they discussed with a studied seriousness.

"Don't change the subject."

"I don't want to talk about this any more." I looked at him, this earnest young man that I loved so dearly. "You're not going to become a Christian are you?"

"I don't know."

"But it's not an idea you would reject out of hand?"

"I thought you would welcome it if I took Communion..."

"Oh yes... Of course..."

I was not sure about this. What if Christianity was a pack of lies and prevarications? If it was I wouldn't want to be part of it any more. I couldn't pay lip service to it because of family sensibilities. I would have to uphold my principles.

"I want to marry in church. I want Matthew to marry us."

"Of course... He's not going to be happy if you took Communion as lip service."

"I know, he told me."

"There you are then. Registry office."

"We'll see. What would you say if I... if I made a commitment?"

"What to?"

"The church?"

A month ago I would have felt glad if Cain had wanted to join the church. It would have solved so many problems, made us just one happy family. But now I was becoming unsure about my belief in the church.

"If you want to take Communion you'll have to talk to your father."

"I'm twenty-one. I can believe what I like."

"And there'll be a terrible argument..."

It was silly to argue about religion. So strange my relationship with Cain. We started out with one person a Christian and one person an atheist and ended up the same, but with the roles reversed. But then I am no longer a pure atheist, I'm a Liberal Rationalist.

"Cain?"

"Yes?"

"It's going to be all right isn't it?"

"What?"

"If we have different beliefs."

"We're not in a position of knowing exactly what our beliefs are."

"But it could lead to differences... of opinion..."

"Are you saying you want to defer the wedding?"

"No. No. I don't want to do that."

I leant my head on Cain's chest. Those familiar man-smells that I had become so accustomed to. Cain held me in his arms and kissed my forehead. It was at that point that Robbie came in. Rudely. Abruptly.

"Ah, caught you at it."

I disengaged myself and looked at him in the entrance-way, framed by the two birch trees in the garden.

"What are you doing here Robbie?"

"Thought I'd pop in and see you. Wanted to have a word with Pater actually. In the house is he?"

Robbie was in his youthful arrogant phase. His use of the words Pater and Mater was just so... so pretentious. He'd dressed himself up like a cheap hood out of the movies. He said he was given the clothes by the proprietors of second hand shops, but I'm sure he stole them.

"Yes," I told him.

"They're coming down soon with afternoon tea," explained Cain.

"Ah, sausage rolls."

"Brandy snaps."

"Oh. I've just learnt a trick with seven cards." He pulled his worn pack of cards from his pocket.

"That's interesting." To my intense annoyance Cain was always trying to ingratiate himself with Robbie.

"You can't let Mother see you with cards Robbie."

"Suppose not." He put the deck away. "I heard a story about Old Mother Goose."

"I don't want to hear it if it's risqué."

"Oh it's very."

"I don't want to hear it then." I looked at him, wondering why he was here. He was always away, God knows where, on Sunday afternoons. "I thought you'd be with Jimmy Peabody."

"Not really."

"Oh no?"

Robbie came into the room. He took off his cap and shuffled his feet. "He's been arrested. He did a burglary."

"A burglary. You're lucky you didn't get caught too."

"I wasn't there Sister. I don't do burglaries. Peabody is a fool. He broke into the Bainbridge's house and left fingerprints all over the place. Stupidity."

"So when you burgle a house you'll wear gloves will you?"

"I'm not going to be burglaring any houses."

"I'm glad to hear that Robbie... I think your father was concerned..." said Cain.

He had to butt into matters that did not concern him. I found this very annoying. Perhaps one day Cain would be an official member of the family and would have the right to comment.

"This is a family matter Cain," I said.

"Don't be so stuffy, sister." Robbie seemed to read my thoughts. "Cain is Brother-in-law." He sat on the wicker chair with a thump. "If I was going into crime I wouldn't go burglaring..."

"But you would go into crime?"

"How could a member of this sanctimonious household go into crime?"

At this point Mother came in with a plate of butterfly cakes. She brushed back a wisp of hair from her forehead and put the plate on the table.

"Robbie? It's nice to see you on a Sunday afternoon." Robbie stood up. She turned her cheek for a dutiful peck.

"There's nothing I'd like more than to spend Sunday afternoons with the family. But sometimes, I get involved in things..."

I was sure I could hear violins playing in the background. Robbie's gushing charm was nauseating, but Mother seemed quite taken in by it.

"Yes dear."

"Butterfly cakes? Where are the sausage rolls Mother?"

"I don't know what that new butcher puts in his sausage meat." Mother looked quite distracted. "I see you've picked some of my flowers Lucy."

"I grew the stocks Mother."

"Didn't you grow the marigolds also dear?" She picked the bunch up from the table and smelt them. "Do you like flowers Cain?"

"Flowers? Ah yes."

"Matthew will be here in a minute. He's making lemonade." Cain moved a chair for her. She sat down, next to Robbie. "Thank you Cain."

Presently Father came in with a jug of lemonade and five glasses on a tray, which he placed on the table. I wondered about the extra glass. Later I realised he would have a reason for knowing that Robbie would be present.

"Ah Robbie, I thought you might be here. Nothing like homemade lemonade. Will you have a glass dear?" Father poured five glasses and passed them around. "Let us drink a toast. To sermons."

We self-consciously drank the toast. "To sermons."

"I must say you were in brilliant form today Matthew," said Cain

"Well that says something, coming from an agnostic."

"Ah yes. Agnostic."

"You'll have to get your father into church more often. Might be able to teach him something eh?"

"Oh he's settled in his ideas."

"He has some good arguments you know. I have to refute them from the pulpit and that's not easy. The birth myths and their meaning. Wrote half of it on Friday morning and then had a mental block. Couldn't get it right. Even prayed for divine inspiration. Then when I was extemporising from the pulpit it came to me in a flash. A light from heaven."

"Impromptu again Matthew. I wouldn't like to lose *Away in a Manger*."

"Of course not my dear. All you have to do is understand the symbol... Now Robbie, I'm glad you're here, we'll have to have a bit of a chat later."

"If it's about my association with a known criminal I don't mind talking about it now Father," said Robbie belligerently.

"What's this about a criminal?" Mother said nervously.

"It's obviously about Jimmy Peabody..." said Robbie.

"Jimmy Peabody... Is that why Mr Peabody came to see you Matthew? Has Robbie been getting into trouble?"

"As far as I know Robbie is not involved..."

"Well that's a relief, I don't know why you permit the association."

"Peabody came to see me this morning about his son. Quite pathetic really. Thought I was some sort of doctor who might cure his family of crime. I showed him the Ten Commandments and told him they were the best medicine. He's a simple man, I suppose the Lord said we should come as children... however I do think we might have a new member in the flock. We can dip the sheep and clip off its woolly dags."

"Well what is this about a crime Matthew?" asked Mother.

"Jimmy Peabody was arrested on a charge of Breaking and Entering with Intent." Robbie explained it carefully, explicitly.

"How terrible. What's this got to do with you Robbie?"

"I had nothing to do with it Mother."

"But you spend all your time with Jimmy Peabody."

"That doesn't mean to say I commit crimes with him. Mother, I want you to know that I'm not going to have anything more to do with the Peabody family."

"Do you really mean that Robbie?"

"It was wrong of me to associate with him." The violins played louder with sweet and sickly intensity. "From now on I'll spend my Sunday afternoons with you."

"I always knew you were a good boy."

"I could have committed a crime with Jimmy Peabody. I realise I was tempted by the Devil, but I'm all the stronger for it. To think I could have set off on a life of... it doesn't bear thinking about."

"You see Matthew, I told you, you should have spoken to him long before now. I never approved of him spending all that time..."

"I spoke to him Millicent."

"Not strongly enough dear. You know what they say if you spare the rod."

"Every person has the right to forge their own destiny. What will be will be. God gave mankind the ability to decide for himself. We are not puppets controlled by the strings of some divine intention. God gave man his freedom and if man decides to sin that is his own responsibility. Except that he must pay the price. God gave man his freedom."

"Freedom to sin!"

He was right you know. Do you wish to hear an argument on causality? Do we come into existence in a flash of God's inspiration or are we a result of natural law? And if it's a natural law is that God or is it just something mechanical? And if it is something mechanical who or what made it, or did it just exist of its own accord?

Come on now, concentrate, don't go to sleep, these are important questions.

But whatever agency it is, does it just sit there and wind up the universe, tick tock, and we are marionettes tied to the mechanism, acting out a prearranged charade for the whole of our lives, or are we the causes of events? Is that bright summer day painted up for our enjoyment or did it, just, happen? These are the thoughts of your last days.

To get back to our story...

"Father did talk to me Mother," said Robbie "I was just too foolish to listen."

"What did he talk about then?

"I always kept Christian ideals before Robbie," said Father.

Cain was embarrassed with this family contretemps. He picked up the plate. "Can I offer you one of your butterfly cakes Mrs Tunnicliffe."

"Why thank you Cain." She took one and held it in her hand not quite knowing what to do with it. "You couldn't have spoken to him very strongly Matthew. All I know is things just don't work out well sometimes."

"But you see Mother, I've learnt my lesson..."

"Don't fret Mother." I had to tell her to calm herself. She looked so upset.

"I'm not fretting. All I know is it's just a mess. Excuse me." She put the butterfly cake down on the table. It went over on its side and one of the wings came off. She went out quickly.

"What's got into the Old Mater?"

"A little touchy today. Excuse me a minute." Father went after Mother.

"Not like the Old Mater to rush off like that. Did I say something wrong?"

"She can see through you Robbie. She can see through you and your crap."

"Clear as a glass, Sister dear, clear as a glass." He was putting on the air of someone absolutely in charge of everything. "Oh well I'll just toddle up to the house and see if I can be of assistance." He went.

"Your mother... Millicent... she seems very anxious..." said Cain.

"It's Robbie..."

"Robbie? It must be a relief."

"What?

"The way he gave up that association."

"He no longer has any use for it."

"But he said he would never commit... a burglary."

"That's what he said. You are stupid to believe him."

Robbie was only seventeen but he'd been given a part and he was bound to play it. Cain didn't understand what I meant. It was his part in The Play. The part of a shyster, a confidence trickster, a dishonest man, a criminal. He practiced telling lies and making his victims believe them. It was something he'd been doing all his life. No, he would never stoop so low as committing a burglary. It would have to be a high class crime because he had been brought up by a high-class family. Mother became upset because she recognised that. Cain wouldn't believe me because he was too good a man and was never cynical enough to consider faults in others. But you see, we are given our parts and we are ordained to play them.

"If you say so. Will you have a butterfly cake?" Cain had to humour me. I know he was being patronising but I found it very hard to get angry with him.

"I will have one, seeing as there are no brandy snaps."

"Or sausage rolls."

"Or sausage rolls."

5

It was those meetings in the garden house that led me to become a Rationalist. I was so earnest about my beliefs in those days. I had found a whole new world of thought and I wanted to cry it out from the rooftops. Here was the golden El Dorado of knowledge and everybody had to know about it. And I was so sure that these ideas were the final and definitive truth about the matter. It was only later in life that I began to question them. To accept that I might have been impetuous. But by then the damage had been done.

Most people are dogmatic when it comes to religion. It's the same with politics. Nothing can be done to change their beliefs. Take my friend Fred Robottom, the President of the Rationalist Society who came to visit the other day. Fred's a good solid man. He wears horn-rimmed glasses and a bow tie because he believes a President has to look the part. He also has a waistcoat with a watch and chain in the fob pocket. You might think that he's somewhat radical, being a Rationalist, but no, he's very conservative. So conservative that he would never admit to the faintest possibility that there could be something in religious philosophy. We sometimes have arguments about that. His problem is he took a stand and stuck to it, the rock of... no that's hardly appropriate is it? But if he ever found that there was a fact in the Bible that he couldn't demolish with some sort of pseudo-logical argument his whole world would crumble and decay. He would become a gibbering wreck. You see, fixed in his ideas. I don't know why he's like that. Perhaps he had an unhappy childhood. Perhaps, like all of us, he needs a solid thing to build his house on.

Later in life I abandoned my fixed ideas on Rationalism. I tried to reconcile the various points of view. After all several members of my family had strong beliefs in Christianity. They were intelligent people and their faith sustained them.

I have since had some thoughts concerning spiritual matters but they fall very far short of explaining the whole thing. I sometimes wonder whether God really is behind it at all. Well if I do get to go Up There and meet the old bugger I'll tell him a thing or two. I would certainly suggest a few organisational changes Down Here. Pity He couldn't come and tell us what His marvellous Creation is all about. I mean we're told that if we be good He'll look after us. But what is 'good?' You would be justified in thinking that life is 'a tale told by an idiot', in which case God is an idiot. Then maybe we're put here to see if we can make some sense out of it. Perhaps it's a puzzle to be solved, and when we've done that the game will be over and everything will disappear into thin air. Do you think that's the reason? Perhaps all these foolish and trivial things like life and love and cruelty and passion are put here to divert our attention from the true mystery. On the other hand perhaps we are meant to know nothing, perhaps we are dumb animals and it is God's intention that we remain ignorant.

I'll tell you a story about ignorance. About ignorance and omniscience. We have a nurse here called Brackwell. Everyone calls her 'Brackish'. She's starchy, inflexible, doesn't like my liberality and complains to Doctor Rogers because I'm still here. Fact is we don't get on at all. I don't think she gets on with the other nurses either. The other day she took a turn, went all dizzy, said she'd had a strange reaction. So they took her away for Tests. Then I noticed that one of my cookies was gone. She'll be admitted somewhere and be kept there for Observation. Ignorance you see. She would have thought they were normal cookies. If I tell them what happened they'll take them away and I won't be able to float through a bad day. But I can't leave a poor creature in distress can I? I'll put a note in the bag. Where is my pencil? *"These are hash cookies. Eat at your peril. Brackwell took one."* They'll find it when I go. Oh I'm sure there will be an Investigation as to how they got here, but it will be too late to discipline me then. I'm God in this situation, I know all about a mystery and nobody else does.

Did I drop off? I must have, just for a minute. I must stay awake. No time for catnaps.

I seem to remember a strange dream. I was in a cathedral. It was cold and misty and I could hear an organ playing, although I couldn't determine where the sound came from. There was a coffin on a marble slab surrounded by six burning candles. A cadaverous man was leaning over the coffin rubbing his hands together and saying "Beloved Son". I looked into the coffin and saw myself lying there surrounded by lilies. They gave off a sweet, sickly, cloying odour. Just like the beautiful vampire girl in the coffin in those old black and white movies. Makes you shiver.

What time is it? My watch is in the bedside cabinet. Midnight. The time when the graves give up their dead to walk in the eerie dew-drenched night.

I know they are here around me, listening and waiting; Mother, Cain, Father, Robbie.

They never say anything, but it is a comfort to know they still live, somehow, and care about me. I long to be where they are. Just a figment of the imagination you might say, or a psychological necessity to resolve the fear of the last days.

But I am not afraid. I have never been calmer.

Cain, Cain, you went so soon. Why didn't you stay with me longer? I needed someone as sensible as you to temper my intemperate ways.

Are you there? Will I see you again?

I remember the day before we were married when we discussed our philosophical differences. We were sitting under a willow tree on the banks of the river. The summer grass was long, dry, going to seed and full of chirping insects. We had burrowed into it and kissed. We had become lovers by this stage in obscure, clandestine, fumbling ways, but this day we had no passion for each other. A day of peace. The Lord's day.

"So you are to become a Christian and I am to become a Rationalist," I said.

"Yes, it would appear so."

"Aren't you going to try to talk me out of it?"

"No."

"Why not? You know I love an argument."

"It's not something to argue about."

"Not something to argue about!? Your religion!?"

"No. You can only argue with any confidence about more trivial matters."

I looked at Cain. His features were fresh-cut, clean. What you might expect a Christian to look like. He'd always been like that, even in his atheist days. It was the face that portrayed a straightforward and honest nature.

"I can't understand you Cain, your decision is entirely without any logical foundation."

"It's nothing to do with logic."

"Well what is it then?" I remember my attitude at the time. Everything was black and white, and if I thought that black was right then black was right and there was nothing that could possibly persuade me otherwise. "You mean to sit there and say that you are knowingly doing something completely illogical."

"I'm not sure if it's illogical. In spite of what Montague says about conflicts in the gospels it may only seem so. I know how I feel about it."

"Women are supposed to be the emotional ones. Men are supposed to be the logical ones."

"We'll have to be the opposite."

I plucked a stem of grass and tickled his nose with it. "Did you tell your father that you were to become a Christian?"

"Yes, I told him."

"How did he react?"

"He, he tried not to show his emotion, but I could see he was shaken."

"What is he going to do?"

"He very magnanimously says that I have the right to believe anything I wish to and that he would defend that right to his last breath. He got that from Voltaire."

"And he needs somebody to mind the store."

"Well I have to mind the store. How can I get a job in this economic depression?"

"But you really want to mind it."

"If it wasn't for conflict, and disappointed looks. I am so sorry for him. His ambition was to have a Rationalist son and now that will never be. I gave him such a blow. I felt like recanting on the spot to make him happy. But I can't. Why does it have such an effect? He's not well you know."

"Not well?"

"He won't admit it. He hides it from everyone, but I think it's serious. He wants us to come and live with him. When I told him about your... views he perked up considerably."

"I like your father. And I like the house."

"That's settled, we'll live there."

It was a plain, comfortable, three bedroomed cottage built of native timbers about the turn of the century. And there was good garden space. I was thinking that Rationalism meant so much to Montague. His personality was based upon it. But I couldn't say that to Cain.

"He has strong ideas..." I said at last.

"Yes." He looked at me. His dark brown eyes were moist. Almost in tears. "We all have strong ideas. Why can't they always be the same?"

"Because they are different."

"But there's only one that's right."

"And we don't know which."

"We think we know. I think I know. Are we going to part because we have different beliefs?" He looked at me so forlorn.

"No!" Of this I was sure. Of our love and our life together I was sure.

"We'll make it out together. We have to."

"Yes." He looked away down the river absently. I had such certainty that I needed this man. "I do want to carry on the family business," he said at last. "At least Montague and I agree on that."

He looked so innocent, lying with his back against the trunk of the tree. I kissed him on the cheek. "Are you worried I might lose my everlasting soul?"

"No. A soul as everlasting as yours will never get lost. When I get up to heaven I'll put in a good word for you."

"You'll have to get there before I do." But an atheist doesn't believe in heaven. "I don't think the Devil would put up with me anyway." It all seemed so incongruous. "We are going to be married in church. Father will marry us."

"Of course."

"Then I'll tell them."

"What?"

"That I'm an atheist."

"After we're married?"

"Yes."

"Couldn't you just... couldn't you just be an atheist in your heart and pretend you're a Christian."

"What a stupid thing to say Cain. You know I have to be myself."

Cain and I were married in Father's church. Montague was in attendance. It was a wonderful day. I forgot that I was a Rationalist and remembered my love for poor, ugly Jesus and the day when he had taught me to play the fiddle. I had the feeling that he was looking down on me from the rafters with kindly benevolence but, of course, I put that down to imagination.

It was after I was married that I told Father of my change in beliefs. I'd popped into his study one day while he was struggling with his sermon. It was very much Father's study and his personality pervaded it. He was sitting at the mahogany desk on his battered leather swivel chair. The walls were crowded with bookcases and pictures of holy places in Israel. The room smelt of cigar smoke. Father smoked no more than one cigar a day and this sanctuary was the only place in the house where Mother permitted him to smoke it. He looked up from his work and waved me into the guest chair.

"I need some help with this."

"Your impromptu sermons are best."

"I got into trouble with my last one."

"Oh?"

"While you were away on honeymoon. I misplaced my papers, brought along the sermon from the previous week. I decided to extemporise on 'fundamentalism and the Bible.' I'd been thinking about it recently. There was an outcry and a Meeting was held. Old Jacoby threatened to write to the council to ask to have me replaced. Ah, if only they could see the light."

"Some of your views are, unconventional."

"Yes, the views of Jesus were unconventional in his time. He threw over the tables of the money-changers in the temple. Right there on the Royal Porch. Montague says I'd make a good Rationalist. Maybe he is right. Even so I seem to be able to remain a good Christian. I think if Christ had come into our church today he'd have got angry and overturned the tables of some of the... ah... fundamentalists. You can only take it so far Lucy, you can only change the cast of bigoted thought in such small increments."

"If at all," I replied.

There were things on his mind, that was clear. He idly picked up the port decanter from its usual place on the window ledge at the far side of the desk. Port was for guests in the study, or for the reviving of hysterical women when they fainted. Father always asserted that port was as effective as brandy in such situations.

"There's so much fundamentalism in the Bible itself. I mean seven creatures of each kind walking onto the Ark. You can't believe that. And the fallacy of the Virgin Birth that the Roman Catholic Church embellishes and perpetuates. People have faith in these icons. They come to mean more than the truth itself. Christ is a living being. He still lives on in the church in spite of the incomplete and shoddy message we receive from the Gospels. I often think of leaving the church and preaching my own gospel, but then would anyone listen?"

"Probably not."

"No. If you want to change things, change them from the inside. I'm sorry if I preach."

"Oh I love hearing you preach."

This was true. I did love hearing him preach. And often what he preached was so close to my Rationalist views. I looked at him carefully. He seemed to be poised, waiting for me to say something.

"I've become a Rationalist," I said at last.

"I thought you might," he said calmly.

"You're not surprised?"

"I'm not blind you know. I know when my nearest and dearest are going through a crisis of thought."

"Cain's become a Christian."

"Cain was always a Christian. Right from the moment I first saw him. I didn't do anything to change that."

"And I was always a Rationalist?"

"I think you might have been."

"You lose one and you gain one."

"I'd never lose you my dear. You are not a losable person. But you see, even though you're a Rationalist, you have Christ in your heart. I can see that."

"To the degree that I owe him something."

"We are always in his debt." He turned back to the papers on his desk and made a note. "You've given me an idea for the sermon. Nothing is ever lost."

"Will you tell Mother?" I asked.

"Something she won't want to know." He mumbled, as though it was something he didn't want me to hear.

"I'll tell her myself."

"No." There was pain in his eyes. "I'll have to do that."

He looked so forlorn, distant, unhappy. Was there something here I didn't know about..

"What's the problem about telling Mother?"

"Millicent isn't well. Her nervous disposition..."

"She's always had a nervous disposition."

He swivelled in the chair and looked at me, straight in the eye. "I'm worried about your mother. I have to tell you things are not altogether all right."

"What do you mean?"

"I don't know. It seems to be... possibility of a mental problem."

"Don't be silly. Mother's always been fussy. I imagine she's going through the change of life. I'll tell her myself."

"No. No, let me do it." He turned back to his desk. "Now this is an interesting idea, if I can develop it."

I left him to his sermon.

Are you there Mother? I can see you, a grey ghost in a white gown, holding a bunch of lilies in your arms. You caress them as you would a baby.

Those are your flowers and you have picked them.

"As you sow, so shall you reap..."

Was it my fault what happened? Do you blame me?

Where are you? Why do you look away?

Are you happy? Are you sad?

Mother and I were in the garden. The roses needed to be deadheaded. That is, trimmed of dying and dead flowers so those fresh and bright ones would be displayed to greater advantage. It was a warm day at the end of summer and we both wore straw hats with ribbons. It was Mother's custom, I remember, to always have a ribbon on her hat while gardening. It's a trivial custom I always followed in later years. Mother and I both had clippers but only she wore gardening gloves.

"Aren't you going to wear gloves Lucy?"

"No, I love the feel of plants."

"Pricks can go septic very easily. Mrs Jones had to go to the doctor after picking blackberries without gloves."

"I'm too pure to go septic."

"I'm sure you are dear."

Personally roses are not my favourite flower. They are too cloying in their beauty and too dangerous with their thorns. Even so I have five roses growing in my garden. All planted in memory of those who have departed. The first was for Montague, who died not long after Cain and I were married. It was an Alba rose, the ancient White Rose of York, the emblem of Richard the Third. After Richard was defeated at Bosworth Field there was a reconciliation between the two warring families, just as there has been a reconciliation between my family and Cain's family... "Plant a black rose to remember me," Montague had said. "Black for the darkness of the soul." I planted a white rose for the hope of purity in his soul. And I planted the rose of a king. Montague and I became very close in his last days. It was such a comfort to him that I had become a Rationalist and because of this he willed the house to me. Cain and I lived in it all our lives.

"There are aphids," I observed as I was clipping.

"I'll spray with soapy water later," replied Mother.

Mother was so serene in the garden. I decided to tell her.

"I've become a Rationalist."

"Yes dear, Matthew told me." She was very calm, yet as she clipped a flower slipped from her fingers and fell to the ground.

"You don't mind?"

"Of course not. It's perfectly all right. Matthew explained it's very modern to have liberal ideas. Believe whatever you want to believe dear."

"You're not upset then?"

"Why should I be upset? You have your life to live. Its perfectly understandable... I'd like to have a statue of Christ in the garden."

"A statue of Christ?"

"Yes. On the cross."

"Would it be appropriate in a garden?"

"Oh yes, he lived in an agricultural district you know. I'm sure it was a crown of rose-thorns they placed on his brow. That's why the flower is such a lovely red colour, don't you think so?"

"The Bible didn't say it was a crown of roses."

"No, perhaps not. It might have been the white Tea rose for purity. Or was it red for blood? What a pity we can't all be pure and yet have children. Can you hear the cello?"

She was in one of her fretful moods. I couldn't understand the conversation. "No."

"Someone is playing on the other side of the hedge. Can't you hear it? It's the Elgar."

"With a full orchestra?"

"No, just the cello part."

"I can't hear anything Mother." She must have been hearing things.

"Oh dear, it's gone now." She looked at me with a look of complete weariness, of complete sadness. "Will you finish these dear. I'm a little tired. I think I'll have a lie down."

We spend all our lives in earnest discussion, trying to reach the answer to various questions of moment, but in the end it is our emotions that sway our decisions. It is our feelings that make us become what we are.

Where are you Mother?

Are you happy?

Are you sad?

I shouldn't have told you, I shouldn't have...

We sin... we pay for it...

Is there any resolution in our days here on Earth?

Is there any resolution?

Robbie... Are you in heaven or are you in hell?

He once told me there was no God in this universe...

Robbie. Robbie... Are you in heaven or are you in hell? I think you should be in heaven.

Mother had made cupcakes and asked me to take afternoon tea to Robbie in his room. I had to give a password at the door and it was a full minute before he let me in. Hiding nefarious things away I assume. Robbie always kept his room tidy. There were pictures of film stars and motor cars on the walls, and men's magazines carelessly strewn about. He was wearing a grey silk shirt.

"Mother asked me to bring it," I said putting it down on the sideboard.

"Stay," he replied. "Cupcakes and coffee. Such depravity. Well Sister I hear you've joined the ranks of the heathen."

"What do you mean?"

"Old Pater tells me you've become an atheist."

"A Rationalist."

"Is there a difference?"

"A Rationalist is someone who uses reason rather than emotion in reaching her conclusions."

"Bit of a sock in the eye for Old God eh, sitting up there on his fluffy little cloud. Pretty soon no-one will believe in Him and He'll disappear in a puff of smoke."

"You always were blasphemous. At least I've given the matter a considerable degree of thought and come up with the only opinion that conscience will allow."

"Conscience. Conscience. Don't mention obscene words in front of me Lucy."

"Well what opinion do you have on the matter?"

"I'm an atheist. There's no God in this universe, there's only dust, there's only clay. There's no soul nor spirit either, not in you or me or any other creature that slithers over the surface of the world."

"Why are you so cynical?"

"Because I want to have a sweet life."

"And a sour death?"

"When that comes I'll be non-existent, so there will be nothing to worry about. I'm here to enjoy the pleasures of life and that is what I shall do while I have the time. I have the means to do it."

"Your means are dishonesty."

"At least I am not as sanctimoniously honest as you are. At least I have the sense not to make a big issue out of my beliefs in front of Mater and Pater."

"Because they'd disown you."

"No, because it would hurt them."

"Oh so there is a little bit of good in him after all." I was getting so angry with Robbie.

"Why do you hate me so much?"

"I don't hate you."

"Oh yes you do. I try my best to be nice to you but it doesn't seem to make any difference."

Robbie had plied me often with his sweet talk. I wasn't going to be taken in by that. Compliments and lies made to influence me. That was Robbie's way with words. I could see through that. He was a turd in a violin case. I decided to turn the conversation back to him. Of course now that he knew that it didn't work he could be as unpleasant as he liked.

"Where did you get that shirt from?" I asked.

"This shirt? Trading."

"Thieving you mean."

"I don't know how many times I've told you, I don't thieve. Only fools thieve. It's too easy to get caught. I trade. I wheel and deal. Even in times like this there's a living to be made if you're sharp enough."

"Oh yes, you are very sharp."

"As a knife." He picked up the cupcake. "We're not much of a family for a bunch of Christians are we?"

He was right. We were once so together and happy in the old days. I remembered the story about the snake in the Garden of Eden. As children we are innocent. As we grow older we partake of the apple and that leads us to a familiarity with good and evil. Things can never be the same again. We have lost that primeval innocence when we obtain knowledge.

"We could be."

He swallowed the piece of cake he was munching. "Pater tells me that Mater got upset when you told her."

"She didn't seem upset at all. Mother is very inflexible in her thinking..."

"You should take her flowers."

"Flowers? What do you mean, flowers? She has a garden full of flowers."

busy life, I've taught a lot of people a lot of things. There's something there to celebrate. Just as long as they say nice things...

I asked Anne if there could be brandy snaps at the supper. She buys them in a shop you know. There's a recipe in my old Edmonds cookbook. I told her to use that. Whether she will or not I just don't know. And I must have the right music. I told her the Air from the third suite by Bach just before the service starts. You know the piece. It's called Air on a G String but it's much better played as he originally wrote it. That'll put them in a suitably reverent frame of mind while they sit and shuffle in silence on their hard wooden seats. And I think we can end up with something frivolous like 'Didn' he ramble?'. Well I never did ramble but I like the song.

Ceremonials, pomp and circumstance, they are important. We have ceremonies for all parts of our lives, death, marriage, birth. Living is a ceremony also.

The other thing Anne has to do for me when I'm dead is to plant a rose beside the five other roses of remembrance in my garden. I have chosen a Rosa Mundi. Why? Firstly it was a bud sport from the Apothecary's Rose, which is Mother's rose. Then the name means 'rose of the world' which describes me, being a worldly wise person. And it is the most beautiful rose, a variegation of red, pink and white, no two flowers the same.

There is a sad story associated with the Rosa Mundi. The King of England was in love with a beautiful young maid called Rosamund. However it was necessary for him to marry a European princess. Political reasons you know. The Princess became jealous and had Rosamund put down. The King ordered that the rose be planted on her grave and there it blooms to this day.

You believe me? I heard part of the story from somewhere... from over the hills... somewhere... far away... The rest of it I made up.

My fist-born was Luke. When he was a baby I would sit by his cot and wonder what sort of man he might become. A little helpless bundle of flesh that was completely dependent upon me for its welfare. And yet he contained within himself the potential for his whole future. The seed of an entire universe of invention. Would he end up in prison, in a lunatic asylum, or in the houses of the great? To make a mark on the malleable clay of the world? Or to live and die in a day of mediocrity, to be a hardly noticed ripple in the river of mankind's remembrance?

But then, that last is the fate of most who are born.

As a wee child Luke was the joy of my life. Mother would look at him in his little knitted vest and say "As bright as a button" or "As sharp as two pins." I sometimes thought that a son should be like his mother, strong-willed and outgoing, but no, he was always quiet and studious, always with his nose in some book, or away day-dreaming among the clouds. At school Luke was a bright student but was never persistent or ambitious enough to make full use of his talents. That's the environment of schools. They are only able to teach that which has already passed the test and been included in the canon of knowledge. Looking forward to new worlds is not part of the curriculum and hence mediocrity is enhanced and imagination inhibited.

He went off to university and ended up playing the trumpet in a jazz band with Dave Lawrence. He was a beatnik too. Beatniks were the version of *La Boheme* before hippies and flower power took over. They lived from what they got by playing pool and the money they stole out of the milk bottles. I never approved. Well I did approve in a way, it's more creative than being a bank clerk. God knows what I'd have done if my son had been a bank clerk. They got up to all sorts of things. I knew some of it. I don't want to know the rest.

He got married, settled down, gave up jazz and bohemianism and worked as a teacher for ten years. They had two girls, my grandchildren, and then got divorced. I never got on with his wife. After they parted she married a computer consultant. That says it all. I hardly ever see the girls.

"She got annoyed at me for not applying for the headmaster's position," he said to me shortly afterwards as though that was sufficient reason for getting a divorce.

"Why didn't you?"

"I couldn't do it. I get depressed sometimes Mum. I couldn't take on the responsibility of being headmaster."

"For goodness sake why do you get depressed? Surely there are enough things in this world to make you happy."

I remembered that I was depressed when I was nineteen years old. The world seemed hard, dark, no use or purpose to anything. '…stale, flat, unprofitable seem to me the uses of this world…' as Shakespeare put it. But after that I had too much to do to get melancholy. Luke looked at me with those soft brown eyes that he had inherited from Cain and recited to me the poem:

"The world is full of such a number of things
I'm sure we all should be as happy as kings."

But are kings happy? 'Uneasy is the head that bears the crown.' It is a mantle of power that ambitious men covet and would want for their own. A prize at the fairground coconut shy. So if your aim is true, a head will fall. I never sought power. It is a bubble with rainbow colours which might be pricked by any contrary wind. I would prefer to be modest and happy than powerful and unhappy. Power and wealth do not generate happiness. Happiness is when you find the flow, when you are in consonance with the pulse of the universe. Did I say that? What a pompous way of describing the Tao.

Why does Luke get depressed? It may be that he suffers from a worm in the mind, like Mother did. It may be that he thinks too much, that he is too sensitive to the ills of the world, like she was. Perhaps I passed onto him a wayward gene that came from her.

He lives on a commune now with a woman half his age. He doesn't want to do much except garden and commune with nature. They grow marijuana in the bush. The sale of it keeps them in bully beef. Highly illegal but why should growing a natural herb be against the law? Still the illegality keeps the price up. I told him one day I wanted to try it out. Even a grandmother can try something new, something a little risqué. We sat in the garden and shared a joint and entered that dreamy world of intensified vision. He brings me cookies now. You can't smoke in a place like this and I've found they ease the aches in this old body of mine. Cookies are better than cigarettes. They last longer and allow you to cruise along.

The picture of a life on a thumbnail. It's like all lives isn't it? You have such high ambition for your children, thinking that they will do so much better than you. Then they gravitate towards mediocrity. At least with Luke it isn't mediocre mediocrity, it's mediocrity with a bit of class.

What else can I say about a person I love as much as any other?

Luke was christened, during the Sunday morning service, in a beautiful white christening gown embroidered by Mother. I had supplied insufficient nappies and he wet himself in Father's arms. Robbie had said he would be there but he had not arrived. He rarely came to church any more. After the service we went to the manse for a small celebration. Mother and I put Luke down in the old cot in their bedroom.

"So nice to have a child in the house again," she said as she tucked him under his little blanket. She and Father were now rattling around alone in the large empty house. "He's beautiful, darling. Go to sleep baby. The men are in the library with champagne."

"He's sound asleep."

"He's a sweet one. He'll break all the young girls' hearts one day"

"I could sit and watch him forever."

"You don't think he'll wake?"

"Never."

"Don't say things like that. Of course you'll wake wee baby. Of course you'll wake."

"Come on let us join the men." I hadn't meant to imply that Luke would never wake up. Mother was becoming strange sometimes, so sensitive to such idle words in a conversation.

Cain and Father were in the library with a bottle of champagne. It had been placed in one of Mother's cake mixing bowls which was filled with ice.

"Ah, is young Luke asleep?" asked Father looking at the champagne as though he didn't quite know what to do with it.

"Like a little lamb," replied Mother.

"He's a very docile child," said Cain to Father.

Father picked up the bottle. "Now that I have a bottle of champagne I don't know how I'm supposed to open it."

"Are we going to wait for Robbie, dear?" asked Mother.

"He just rang in. He has some problem with a business transaction. He said he'd come on later."

"Why is he always so unreliable? I don't understand why he has to do business transactions on a Sunday."

"It's his way of life dear. 'The Sabbath is made for man, not man for the Sabbath'." Father had removed the wire from the cork and was not quite sure exactly what to do next. "Saved a shilling a week out of my stipend for this. Never opened a champagne bottle in my life. There's morality for you."

"Let me, Matthew," said Cain.

Father gave the bottle to Cain who quickly had the cork popping up to the ceiling and the first froth of bubbles captured in a wine glass. (The manse didn't run to champagne glasses). Cain passed the bottle back and Father poured into four glasses.

"Robbie will have to drink his flat. That's the disadvantage of being late. Champagne has to be poured fresh from the bottle, isn't that so?" He handed us each a glass. "Ah-ha. Always said I'd have the best French champagne on the day I christened my first grandson. To young Luke."

We all drank the toast. Mother gave a grimace. She coughed and spluttered on the wine, spraying droplets onto the tablecloth.

"Did it go down the wrong way Millicent?" asked Father.

"I'm not used to sparkling wine Matthew."

"There's nothing wrong with a drop of wine occasionally. The Lord himself would participate, especially at Communion eh? His enemies even called him a glutton and a wine-bibber."

"Of course not. He turned the wine into water before he drank it."

What was Mother thinking of? I changed the subject. "Did he really wet during the baptism Father?"

"I believe a small damp patch. I usually advise the mothers to use a double set of nappies."

"You didn't advise me."

"No. Somehow one expects members of one's own family to know. Short-sighted of me of course. We'll remember next time. I never knew a baby that didn't get excited at their christening. One feels the spirit of the Lord descend. Just an idle fancy perhaps."

We heard a bang at the front door and then the sound of the door slamming shut.

Mother looked nervous. "Is that someone at the door?"

"Robbie I imagine dear."

Robbie came into the room. He was abrupt, wild-looking. He wore expensive clothes as usual but they were ruffled, dishevelled.

"Robbie, you've come at last.".

"Sorry Mother, something cropped up."

"Well give your mother a kiss then." Robbie presented the side of his face and held his breath. I could guess he'd been drinking. Mother pecked at his cheek. "Are you not well?"

"Perfectly well."

"Well how about a glass of champagne?" Father picked up the bottle.

"Champers eh? I won't say no." Father poured him his glass. "Well, here's to my beautiful young nephew. Cheers." He drank it down in one gulp. "Say this is good stuff. You'll have to keep on having babies, Sister."

"Robbie, have you been drinking?" asked Mother.

"No, of course not. Where would a thirsty man get a drink on a Sunday, unless he were to go to Communion, or to a christening?"

"Give me the glass." Father took the empty glass from Robbie's limp fingers and placed it on the table beside the bowl of ice. "What's this all about son?"

Robbie slumped down in a chair. He suddenly looked so helpless, like an unfledged youngling bird that had been thrown from the nest.

"Can you lend me a quid Father?"

"A pound note? What do you want a pound note for?"

"I've paid you back in the past."

"That doesn't answer my question."

"I need it."

"Have you been lending Robbie money Matthew?" Mother was clutching her shawl. Her knuckles were white.

"Just a small loan some years ago dear, to set him up in business. He repaid the sum with interest."

"Will you lend me a quid Father? Please?"

"There's money in the collection," said Father. "About a pound I would think."

"You can't interfere with the collection," said Mother.

"We have a few pounds in our account. I'll go to the bank tomorrow."

The colour was coming back into Robbie's face. He squirmed in the chair, looked angry. Aggressive. Dangerous. Father went to the study where he kept the collection.

"I don't understand what this is about Robbie." Mother was clutching at her shawl as though it was her salvation. "Why would you need money all of a sudden? You never tell me about your business but you always seem so well off, even in these times."

Robbie stood up. "My assets are tied up. Now Mater I would very much like to have a look at that young nephew of mine. Will you show him to me?"

Robbie put his arm around Mother's shoulder. She seemed to relax. A secret smile of gladness at the thought of Luke and of Robbie's fondness for him. "Yes. You'll have to be quiet, he's fast asleep."

Mother and Robbie went.

"What's this all about? Why does he need money in such a hurry?" asked Cain.

"He's been caught out," I told him.

"What do you mean?"

"He's been caught out in one of his confidence tricks."

"Confidence tricks? I don't know anything about confidence tricks."

Valerie Johnson, a widow on one of the church committees, had confided in me. What a genial and charming young man Robbie was, and the son of the vicar. She gave him some money to invest in a highly unlikely scheme concerning cigars imported from Cuba. After a few months he told her there had been a change in Government regulations and the deal had fallen through. She got half her money back. After all there were expenses and overheads. She wasn't too sad. She was wealthy and lonely, and Robbie was a congenial companion. And I'd seen him in the company of other wealthy women and even the occasional businessman.

"He's been fleecing rich widows for ages. He puts up get rich quickly schemes for those with more money than sense. I hear all about it from the people involved," I told Cain.

"I don't believe Robbie would do such a thing."

"You are so naive sometimes. You have been taken in by his carefully calculated veneer of charm. Believe me, I know Robbie."

"I know what you're saying, but basically Robbie is a fine person. Even if he is a criminal, he's honest about it."

Robbie came back.

"Still fast asleep?" I asked.

"He woke up. What a pong when they do their business. I had to let Mother deal with it," said Robbie. "Grown a bit since I last saw him hasn't he."

"Yes. Babies do."

"Funny little things. You touch his tootsies and he smiles. I wouldn't mind having one myself one day." Robbie looked somehow relaxed. The smile of a baby still lodged in his heart.

"If you find a wife that will have you," I said.

"A wife? Yes, now that's a thought."

Matthew returned with a bag full of coins.

"Sorry for the delay. Ah, received a telephone call. Here's your money. Count it if you like. Where's Millicent?"

Robbie took the money. "Changing the baby. Thanks. I'd better be off."

"Aren't you going to say goodbye to Mother?" I asked. I was angry with Robbie for treating us like this.

"Yes, stay for a while. I've just heard a story about... ah ha... one you would like," said Cain.

He was always trying to get in with Robbie but was never quite successful. Robbie had Cain worked out. Cain was not at this time a person suitable to be drawn into his world of dark secrets.

"I've seen the baby. Had a glass of champers. What more is there to do?"

"Just wait for your mother," said Father.

"Of course I'll stay a minute for Mother. There's just a pressing appointment..."

"There is something I need to talk to you about, Robbie. While I was out Constable O'Connor rang," said Father.

"Oh yes, what did he want?" Robbie put on an air of nonchalance.

"He wanted to know where you were. Wanted to have a chat. I said you might drop in on him."

"What would I have to say to O'Connor?"

"From what he said I think you will know."

"What do you mean Father?"

Robbie's air of self confidence began to deflate like a balloon when the air is let out. Father looked stern, unsure whether he should say what he was going to say.

"I believe there is a matter here that should be, ah, brought into the light. On three occasions members of the congregation approached me with complaints concerning their association with you Robbie, complaints ah, concerning financial transactions. We discussed it didn't we Robbie. Naturally I had to accept your assurances. But now the police are involved..."

"Well if anyone had anything to complain about they could have come to me and I would have put it right. Are you saying that I didn't tell you the truth? Is that it?"

"My confidants are people I can rely on. We live in difficult times, it is the midst of a depression, yet you always seem to have money, and I've no idea what sort of work you are involved in."

"I work at my business. There are still people who are capable of earning a living. Not everyone is on relief work. You know I can't get to the bank on a Sunday."

"Then I'm sure a quiet chat with Constable O'Connor will sort it all out."

Mother came back into the room.

"What's this about Constable O'Connor?" she asked.

"Nothing Mother."

"You should tidy yourself up. Coming to a christening with your shirt all unbuttoned. Fancy you not knowing how to change a baby's nappy. One day you will have a child and I will have to help the mother."

Robbie looked more and more like a bedraggled bird, trapped in its cage, with no possibility of escape. A change came over him, as though he at last accepted his situation. He placed the bag of coins on the table.

"This money..."

"Yes?"

"It's important, for you, isn't it? Not to take from the church?"

"It's not taken from the church. I can make it up." Father looked at Robbie sadly. I thought of the compassion of Christ. "You know Robbie, it's no use running away from it, whatever it is. If there is a debt to be repaid then it will be repaid."

"Here." Robbie picked up the bag of coins and gave it to Father. "I was going to do a bunk."

"Has my boy been doing something naughty?" asked Mother in a wistful voice.

"Yes. Good-bye Mother, come and see me in jail. The police are after me."

"But I know my little son. He's a good boy really."

Cain picked up his glass and gave it to Robbie. "Have a glass of champagne before you go."

"Thanks Cain." Robbie drank it down in one swallow.

Mother looked quite calm, serene. "What did you do Robbie?"

"You don't need to know."

"Why did you do it?"

"I liked it."

"That's no reason. You don't always do something because you think it's nice. Not if it's bad..."

"So you've always told me."

"Give your mother a kiss." Robbie embraced Mother and kissed her on the cheek. For once I believed he was being true to himself. "You will have to be a good boy now."

Robbie disengaged from Mother, a light in his eyes. The feathers were now bright, brilliant, dark, burning with the fire of his corruption. "I'll never be a good boy Mother."

"No. I suppose not."

"Pray for me if you like."

"I will," said Father..

"Probably won't do me much good."

"You don't know... The power... Give us your hand my boy."

"Do I deserve it?"

"Yes." Robbie and Father embraced. I could not understand how my parents could be taken in by this.

"You'd better go," said Mother..

"Yes. Give us a kiss Sister." I didn't want to kiss him but I knew that if I didn't Mother and Father would be distressed. "You're my conscience you know." There was no possibility that he would worm his way into my affections with statements such as that. I squirmed. He shook Cain's hand. "Just think, if they put me in jail I won't have to fight in any war. Give us a kiss Mother."

"Just go," I said.

Robbie stood there, rooted on the spot. Unable to move. "Go? Yes go." he looked at his wristwatch, and then, he was gone.

Cain sat. I sat. Mother was leaning on Father's shoulder.

"It's all right Millicent".

"No Matthew, it's not all right."

"It will be all right."

"Don't be stupid, how can it be?" She looked at him with moist eyes. "Well tell me. How can it be?"

"It will be."

"Well what are we going to do?"

"Trust in the Lord."

"Trust in the Lord?"

"Yes."

"The Lord has forsaken us. We have sinned against His will." She moved back from Father. "Did you know about this all along?"

"I had some idea."

"Why didn't you tell me then?"

"You know how you worry."

"You shouldn't have kept it from me Matthew. It doesn't matter if I worry. What is there to do?"

"We should have a cup of tea." It was the only thing I could say.

"Tea? After Champagne?" Mother was quite distracted.

"I like Robbie. He is a bit of a card at times. I like him," said Cain.

"The devil has claimed his soul, Matthew. Where were you when he was creeping into our parlour."

"Now Milly," said Father in distress.

"The devil's claimed his soul."

Mother was starting to become agitated. She was being foolish. I had to point that out.

"Don't talk about the devil Mother. You can't believe things like that."

"Now dear, we don't have to discuss this now."

I think Father was sorry he had confronted Robbie with his crooked ways.

"Everything is not all bad. Look at today. A new life has come to the Lord," he said.

"A new life? To what house? To what sort of future? I'm sorry Lucy, I'm sorry Cain. I worry about it all the time."

"We should talk about it if it is a matter of concern. Lucy and I have felt for some time..." Cain just did not understand.

"Thank you Cain. There is nothing you can do about it. People turn their face from God. I'm sorry Lucy. The whole world has become evil. The pus oozes out..."

"There now my darling Milly, there now."

"When I was a child everything was beautiful, everything was perfect. I was happy all the time. A drop of dew on a rose. I married Matthew and it still was beautiful, peaceful. Everything was just right. Then things started to go wrong. Why are we shown the good at the start, to have it torn away later?"

"There now, there now."

"Wars and weapons and murder and torture. Why are there such things in the world? Why does God let such things happen? Why does He allow the devil to exist?"

"It's all right Milly, it's all right."

"Nothing will be any good. Never."

I put my arms around her. "Don't cry Mother, don't cry."

Father knelt in prayer. "May the Lord Jesus Christ preserve us."

"Don't cry Mother. Don't cry."

"I will cry. Nothing will ever be any good any more. Never. Never. Never."

Oh mother, on the day that your first grandchild was taken into the church you loved so much, you found out about the errors in your son, and I discovered the error in your thoughts.

Why should your God lay this affliction upon you?

Is there a God who would permit such distress to invade the mind of one of His own?

I decided that if there was a God then it was not such a one as is described by the Christian Church, but I kept this opinion to myself.

Still, I suppose you can read the book of Job.

Mother, you must have sat beside your own son when he was a baby and wondered what would happen to him as life continued its inevitable path. Yes look what happened to Robbie... Are you happy, are you sad?

Oh Mother, did I hurt you when I naively told you about my change in religious convictions, did that worry you?

Where are you Mother?

Are you happy?

Are you sad?

7

So there really was a problem with Mother's state of mind. Up until then I had merely accepted her eccentricities as being part of her personality. I had completely forgotten the conversation I had accidentally overheard on the Riverbank Day. Mother, always a fusspot, always worrying about something. Mother playing the violin with a look of bliss, carried into another world of sublime serenity. A world she forever sought and never found.

But Mother, there are things in the world that are not quite right and you have to accept them. Didn't Father tell you that? Didn't you learn a lesson from Jesus Christ who consorted with the halt and the lame in body, mind and spirit because he felt he could bring to them a message of redemption? Because they were more in need of his message than the priest in the synagogue.

But what is it that makes us what we are? You might think - 'I am me, and that is my personality, my life. I am owned by no-one.' But then are you? When you came into being in this world you were created by something. Something other than yourself. So, are you yourself, or are you owned by someone else? A pawn of God? Certainly you make the decisions, but is that an illusion? Is that something determined by a higher intelligence before life carved out your presence in this world?

And so I must ask the question: was Mother's illness determined before she came into being on this earth? Was it part of some plan for existence, or was it just an unfortunate accident, an experiment of some almighty God that went horribly wrong, but necessary for the development of the human race?

There is a species of agnostic that assert that God could not exist because of the crooked ways of the world.

Thinking of her in a state like that made me think of Julie. Julie is the 'partner' of Glen, my grandson. She was one of the ten people who came to visit me the other day. Julie's blind, you know, but she doesn't let that affect her. She told me one day she was glad she met Glen because he was someone who would take her out to parties. I like Julie, she's a cheeky little thing, but pretty smart all the same. One other time when she was in a more serious mood she told me she thought it was all right to be blind because it made her try harder. A challenge. She had to look into herself and discover what resources were available to compensate for the loss. That's true you know, I've noticed myself that children of wealthy parents seldom turn out well. Then I read something about cultured abalone. They won't develop properly if they are overfed when they are spawn. You have to have hardship in order to develop yourself to the full. I've seen some people with disabilities just lie down in a sea of self-pity and blame the world for their loss. Have you ever read the book of Job? That's a lesson on coping with affliction.

Julie saw a serious fault in her life and reacted with positive good humour. But Mother saw a flaw in existence and could not cope. Mother had the unreasonable expectation that everything should be perfect. It was a worm in her mind, an inappropriate belief. But then, you see, she had been taught that God was perfect in all ways and could not accept that His creation would contain a flaw.

When I look at creation I see that it contains both good and bad. Then if this creation is the result of One God then He (or She or, more probably, It) must have intended that it contain both good and bad. Or else we had two Gods in conflict, one who created good and one who created bad. You can't have it both ways. You can't have a One God who is perfectly good and yet have evil. Evil must have been God's Intention. It must have been part of His or Her or It's design. Just imagine if everything was absolutely perfect. How bored we would get. There would be nothing to do, nothing to achieve. A perfect world would be the next thing to Hell.

And if we didn't have evil there wouldn't be B-Grade movies. Where would we be without B-Grade movies?

Robbie went to jail. He had embezzled money from a wealthy widow. On the witness stand she apologised to him for being the instrument of his incarceration. It was her son who had made the complaint. Mother and Father visited him in prison. On these occasions Mother always leant on Father's shoulder and always had a handkerchief to her eye. There were mumbles in the congregation but Father took no notice. When my parents asked me why I did not go with them I did not answer because I did not wish to cause Mother any more distress. In those days I did not believe there would be redemption for Robbie. I believed he would reside in hell forever. Mother, on the other hand, held out the hope that he would be saved. She had the compassion, I didn't.

Anne was born two years after Luke. Then my dear husband was conscripted to fight overseas in a war that he believed to be righteous. I was left alone with two young children and a business to manage somehow. I cursed the insanity of Hitler and the fools who wanted to trample over a piece of land and were prepared to kill and maim millions of people to achieve it.

What is the point of that? Our bodies are fragile bubbles which float in the air for an instant of time and then so quickly disappear. And the ownership of the land that has been won with such great expenditure of blood and toil will be taken from the new owners in the end. All that remains from such efforts are graveyards of broken stones and rusted weapons of war. And for the brave soldiers that survive, the fame and renown will trickle through their fingers like grains of dust, as they to dust return.

During the war I took the children to church on Sundays and then to the manse for roast dinner. The children were always very well behaved on these occasions. Father and Mother both had a remarkable way with them. One time that I remember was a family conference, a month after Robbie was released from his first term in jail.

"Did Robbie say that he would come to see us one Sunday, dear?" asked Mother, busily feeding mashed vegetables into young Ann's mouth. Robbie had only come once, to see Mother, when neither Father nor I were there.

"He, ah, I believe... He intended to come to dinner, but some... business... I asked him to come this afternoon."

I could see from his expression that he had some Reason for inviting Robbie that day, and was slightly embarrassed about it. I wondered what it could be.

"He's not still doing... business? I thought he was going to settle down." Father did not reply. "That's a good girl. Eat it all up for Grandmother."

Anne smiled and dribbled down her bib. She banged the tray of the high-chair with her spoon. Luke was sitting up at the table on a cushion on a chair. He was proud of being able to sit up like the adults. Very seriously, and with calm deliberation, he was eating food which Father had carefully cut into small pieces.

"This is a nice piece of beef," said Father, always a fine trencherman when roast beef and Yorkshire duff were concerned.

"Yes dear."

Mother had served herself small portions and hardly ate anything. She had become very thin, almost ethereal, as though there was no substance to her.

After dinner I put Anne down in her bassinette on the big chair in my old bedroom. Father engaged in an earnest conversation with Luke, while Mother and I went into the garden. It was springtime but I noticed this year there were no spring bulbs. Mother had always had bulbs in the past, as I remembered well from the Ugly Jesus Day.

"Where are the daffodils?" I asked.

"I asked Mister Preston to dig them all up."

Mister Preston was a member of the congregation who also acted as Mother's part time, honorary gardener.

"Why did you do that? I love the daffodils."

"Yes, you grow them in your garden dear." Mother looked so frail, exhausted. She sat on the rustic garden seat. "I don't grow them any more."

I sat down beside her and held her hand. "Why is that?"

"Haven't you ever noticed how ugly they become when the flowers die?"

"No I never noticed they were ugly."

"They don't last. Why should a daffodil be so beautiful one minute... and the leaves, they go all brown." Mother took her hand from mine and put it over her heart. "I get palpitations."

"The leaves have to die Mother..."

"Dead leaves are the work of Satan. It was Satan that cursed the fig tree, not Jesus."

"When the leaves die they are composted into the earth for the renewal of new plants."

"I'm sure you are right dear. I never did study botany." Mother looked down at her feet. "Even my stockings are wrinkled." She bent down to straighten them. They were loose about her thin ankles and the wrinkles returned as soon as her fingers left them.

"The decay of leaves really does have a good purpose Mother."

"I know dear." She looked at me with those sad grey eyes. "It doesn't seem to make any difference."

"What do you mean?"

"Matthew explains it to me. He's very good to me you know. I don't know where I'd be without him." She plucked a sprig of rosemary from the bush that was growing from beside the seat and gave it to me. "There's rosemary, that's for remembrance."

As Ophelia said.

"Thank you mother."

"We had rue growing but I pulled it all out. Rue's for sorrow. I'm sorry dear, I'm quoting from Macbeth."

"Hamlet I think."

"Oh yes. Poor Ophelia. She went mad you know. She drowned herself in the brook among the wild herbs. One of them had an improper name. You may remove rue from the garden if you wish but it doesn't remove from the heart."

I put the sprig on my lap and held her hand. "You don't need to worry Mother."

"I know I don't need to dear, but I do... all the time... I worry about everything. Your poor mother is a sick girl Lucy."

"There now."

"It started when that Hitler came along with his tanks and his goose-strutting. I prayed that things might change but God did nothing. Then God gave me a son who did wrong. You see my dear, nothing in this world is right at all."

"But... but there are good things Mother."

She wasn't listening to me. Her eyes seemed to be fixed on the statue of an angel she'd had placed in the garden. But her eyes were actually fixed on far infinity. Her whole mind and spirit seemed to be in another world.

"Matthew keeps telling me. I wish he wouldn't. It won't do any good. I see a spider on a plant and I get terrified. It might come and poison me, or kill a beautiful ladybird."

"Spiders don't eat ladybirds."

"You don't know. You don't know." Her voice was hard, strident, full of anguish. She stood up and started to walk along the path. I went beside her.

"What are we to do?" I asked.

"There's nothing to do. I'm sorry dear. There's nothing to do."

"Of course there is. There must be something."

She leant on my arm. We walked around the garden until we came upon one of her favourite roses. At this time of the year there were no flowers.

"The Apothecary's Rose. It's one of the most celebrated of all the ancient roses." Mother seemed so rise in stature. Her voice took a softer tone. "It's the rose of healing you know. All the apothecary's would have it growing outside their shops. It's painted with the blood of the martyrs. And they made rosaries of the petals"

"There's another story," I said. "It came from Persia and it was a white rose then but it was loved by the nightingale. You remember you told me the story. How the bird crushed the rose with its love and the thorns pierced its breast. Its blood turned the white rose red. So they called it the Red Damask."

"Just a story dear. It was the blood of Christ first, then the blood of the martyrs. The Persians made up the story of the blood of the nightingale because they hated Christians. They were heathens you know." She looked at me with such an air of certainty. "You planted a rose for Montague when he died didn't you?"

"The White Rose of York."

"This is the Red Rose of Lancaster. When I die will you take a bud from it and propagate a new plant? Put it next to the rose of Montague."

"Of course."

"York was Richard the Third. He was an evil man. Lancaster forgave him. I forgive Montague. He was a good man, but it was the snake that led him astray. You'll plant roses around me, for all the family, won't you dear?"

"Of course Mother."

"And lay them on my grave. Lay the blood of Christ on my grave."

We walked back to the house. Robbie was there. He put his arm around her.

"You see, I came at last Mother."

"There's my good boy."

Father was pouring boiling water into the teapot. "Will you have a cup of tea, dear?"

"I'm a little tired. I think I'll take a nap. You don't mind do you Robbie? I'll see you when I wake up. Is little Luke having his afternoon nap?"

"Yes," said Father. "He's on our bed."

"Then I shall join him," and off she went.

Father put the tea things on a tray. "Let us go down to the garden. There's something we need to talk about."

We went to the summerhouse. Father, Robbie, myself. Outside in the garden the sun was bright and the birds were singing but there were few flowers blooming. In my head I could hear the dull drone of aeroplanes rumbling through the war-torn skies of Europe. Reverberations from patriotic movies. They resided in my mind because that was where my thoughts were, in the war where Cain was. Taken to be a soldier in a distant country. I feared that he would die a lonely violent death for a cause that owed him nothing. And there might be no flowers for his grave.

We had come there to discuss Mother. Robbie sat on the wicker chair and said nothing. He could feel my resentment and Father's sorrow. His face was prison-white and his knuckles were prison-blue. Father was nervous and fussed with the teapot.

"Are you drinking tea, Lucy?" he asked.

"Yes. No milk and a slice of lemon please," I replied.

"You've changed the way you take it?"

"It's better for my figure."

Robbie looked up. He put on an air of casual nonchalance. "I can show you a trick with seven cards. I learned it in the boob."

"And tell a dirty story too I suppose," I said.

"Put the deck away." Father picked up the milk jug. "Milk?"

"Two sugars thanks." Robbie's voice was harsh, distant.

"Ah yes." Father was pouring the tea from a blue china teapot. "I prefer milk and, ah one sugar." He passed everyone their cup. There was silence. "You know I've asked you both to come here for a purpose..."

"Why ask me to come?" Robbie's voice had the edge of anger.

"You're a member of the family."

"Black sheep."

Father gave a wry smile. "I'm not going to argue with you over the colour of your wool." Robbie did not think this was funny. He put his cup down in the saucer with an impatient gesture and glared. Father's lips pressed together. "I asked you here to discuss the form I have to sign for the doctors."

"What form Father?" Robbie asked.

The form. The form. He didn't know what the form was. "I have it here somewhere." He put his hands in his pockets searching, searching. "It is necessary for Millicent's, treatment."

"Treatment? What treatment?" demanded Robbie.

"As the next of kin I have the power to approve, however, however, I feel I should discuss the matter with the family..." He looked lost, alone, defeated. "I would have invited Cain of course but he's at the front."

Why did he say that? What relevance?

Robbie stood up and stalked around. "What about Molly, old man? Is she not to be invited?"

Molly was Robbie's common-law wife, the mother of his child. I didn't know what relevance this had either. "What do you mean? Molly? You're not even living together."

"Oh we do occasionally, dear sister."

Father was searching absent-mindedly in his pockets. "If Molly had met the family... Ah here it is." He pulled out a brown envelope.

"What's this all about, Pater?" demanded Robbie.

"It's about mother's illness," I told him.

"Well I certainly don't know anything about any illness mother might have."

"If you hadn't been in jail these last three years then you would have known about it all right. Anyway she came to visit you. You must have noticed something."

"What I see I cannot know, and what I know I cannot tell."

What did that stupid rhyme mean? I was so angry with Robbie. Angry for the trouble and distress he had caused Mother and Father. Angry for things that were never to be forgiven.

"Your mother is suffering from a severe anxiety psychosis," Father said as though he were delivering a sermon.

"Severe anxiety...? I've never seen her in a state of severe anxiety. I mean she does get a bit nervy sometimes..." said Robbie.

"The condition is worse than you think."

"Worse than I think? I saw her the other day. We had afternoon tea..."

"If you'd spent more time..."

"Time. Time. I know about time. I suppose you blame me for it. Going to jail eh? Caused her to become worried..."

"We don't blame you Robbie."

"No, we just think you caused it," I told him.

"That's enough Lucinda. You can't blame any one thing for Millicent's condition, and I don't blame you Robbie." Of course Father was a Christian. It was his duty to forgive.

"No I just caused it," shouted Robbie.

"Robbie!"

"All right. You're the minister of heavenly providence. Why don't you call on the old fellow upstairs to come up with a solution eh?"

"This may be a solution Robbie." Father took a piece of paper from the envelope.

"What is that then?"

"A treatment."

"What treatment?"

"It is absolutely necessary." I knew about the treatment and that it was the only thing available for my poor mother. She who was worried about a spider crawling up the wall and in absolute terror of any mundane event occurring in the world. I could tell from Robbie's attitude that he would not be in favour of it, that he wanted to deny her, that he wanted to oppose what I considered to be her only hope for salvation.

"That doesn't tell me what it is. I assume you have some medical advice."

"Doctor Kukmann. He has all the... qualifications. He was trained in Vienna," explained Father.

"Some quack of a trick cyclist? What do you think of this fellow Lucy?"

"You don't have to be so aggressive." He couldn't expect much support from me.

"All right, I'll be nice and charming shall I? I'll go out and buy you a brandy snap."

"He has the necessary qualifications," I said.

"And I suppose he's a nice fellow."

"He is a bit strange. They all are I suppose," replied Father.

I had to admit it was so. Someone you didn't quite believe could be true. A guttural accent. Rimless glasses. A comic strip character.

"You see."

"It's not a matter of what Doctor Kukmann says or is. The psychiatrist who developed the procedure has won a Nobel Prize. The operation is to be undertaken by a surgeon. It is commonly performed in a number of hospitals throughout the world." Matthew had begun preaching again.

"Operation? What operation?"

"It's quite simple. It was explained to me, just a tiny cut to the brain..."

"You're talking about a pre-frontal lobotomy?"

"Yes I believe that was the term he used."

"Then you're talking about the death of somebody. They put a little knife into the brain and cut out the soul. That's modern psychiatry for you."

"Oh don't be so melodramatic Robbie." I had to tell him that. The image was absolutely ridiculous."

Robbie stood up and started pacing around. He was agitated, angry, but his voice had a resonance and power I had never seen before. If I'd believed in that superstitious nonsense I'd have thought he was speaking the words of the Devil.

"Melodramatic eh? I'll tell you all about it. There was this fellow I met in the boob. His name was John Long. We used to call him Frilly Longjohns because he was fond of taking ladies under-things from off of the washing line. Bit of an agitated nervous fellow, but he could tell a few good yarns. Well he was in and out of boob, in and out of the loony bin, so they did it to him to stop him from being agitated. Thought he might lose the desire for frillys eh? I owed him a fig or two so I went up to see him in the hospital the other day. There was nothing there. You could tap him on the head and you wouldn't even get an echo. An empty man. And I missed out on all those yarns he'd never be able to tell me again. You want something like that to happen to my mother?"

"Is this true?" asked Father.

"Father, you know you can't believe a thing he says," I said in anger.

"This is my son, Lucy."

What son? How could he claim a person like that as a son? What was happening here?

"You know it's the only hope for Mother," I said.

Father looked at Robbie and then me. "When I was first told about the procedure I thought God had come to answer my prayers..."

"Well if God wanted us to have brains with little cuts in them then I'm sure He would have given us them." Robbie knew he had the advantage. But he was Godless.

"What do you know about God?" I asked him.

"As much as you, Sister."

Father folded the piece of paper and put it back in the envelope. "Robbie is right."

"What do you mean Father?"

"About the brains."

"I don't understand you."

"If God had wanted to give us a brain with a little cut in it He would have given us one. In the Gospel of Thomas, one of the Apocrypha, the disciples asked Christ if God meant for the Jews to be circumcised. Christ said they would have been born so if God wanted it."

"What are you talking about? This is the only chance for Mother's recovery and you give us a sermon on circumcision out of some obscure Gospel. What's that got to do with anything?"

"God gave us love, and prayer. Those are the medicines we must use."

"Oh God. Spare me this." I looked at Father. His eyes were determined. He put the envelope back in his pocket. "Are you going to sign the form?"

"No. Never."

"Damn you Robbie. Damn you. I accuse you for the death of my mother. I accuse you." I was so angry with Robbie I threw my cup of tea at him and stalked out. I heard them speak to each other as I walked down the path.

"So there we are Father."

"Yes, there we are my boy."

8

When I was young we sometimes went on Excursions. In common usage the word 'excursion' means 'going out of your way', but the Excursions we went on were special train journeys, ones for occasions not on the normal timetable. For example one might take you to a Spring Fair on in a distant town and bring you back home afterwards. Just for the day. An Excursion always begins with a departure from the railway station and ends with an arrival at another railway station. But life is different, it begins with an arrival at the station and ends with a departure. And in life the Spring Fair occurs in between the arrival and the departure, not the departure and the arrival. No matter whether we travel in life or on a train, time passes and things change. Perhaps the life after death is a train journey. When we die we board the train, sit on the seats and watch the scenery of the world pass by the window until it is time to arrive back at the fairground. At least that's what the gurus in India will tell you. They will tell you that life and death are merely Spring Fairs and Excursions. They will also tell you that existence is merely a ride on a carousel and that you can get off it only if you are high-minded and become one with God. I once studied the thoughts of the Indian gurus with the idea of becoming a Brahman Rationalist. In the end I lost interest. Somehow not the right thing for me. That's not to say there 'isn't something in it.' Perhaps you have to be born in India, or wear beads and flowers.

Life and death are different ends of the same piece of straw. When my visitors came the other day there was an example present of the withered end, someone who was about to depart (myself). There was also an example present someone who had just arrived, Julie and Glen's wee son. A lovely baby just one month old. My great grandson. I was allowed to hold him. He dribbled on my shoulder and I felt the dampness. To think that I was once like that, so soft and warm and helpless. Once I might have dribbled, in the same way, on Mother's shoulder. She would never have felt the dampness of course, she would have placed a napkin to catch the drips. And then there were the times when I had my own babies, dribbling all over me. I so much loved to feel those dribbles. Unlike Mother I'm not a napkin-on-the-shoulder person.

Tracy and Glen have named him Matthew. It was my idea. You have to keep these family names alive. I first suggested Cain but they didn't seem to like that. Nobody gets called Cain unless they have a father with a mordant sense of humour like Montague. And there never was anyone more inappropriately named than my dear husband.

Tracy and Glen are going to have young Matthew christened. I told them that they should get married before the christening. I mean to say how can parents have their child christened if they are not married? They seemed to be surprised at this suggestion. After all, they know I'm a Rationalist, and Rationalists are supposed to be pretty radical. Why should a Rationalist care if people live in sin or not? What I've never told them is that I'm a Liberal Rationalist, which is quite different. Theoretically I don't care if people live together out of wedlock, but in reality I do care. It doesn't seem right and that's just because I've been brought up to think in that way. Living with someone and having children is a thing that requires care and commitment. If you are going to do that then you should state your intentions clearly to each other and in public. It's the reason for the marriage ritual. Being together with your partner is not something you can take lightly.

Someone once told me that all children who weren't christened automatically went down to hell when they died. That's the mythology of religion. This person was a raving fundamentalist who I'd met at the launch of a book by a liberal American Bishop. I asked her what about a Hottentot who's never heard of Christ? Would a Hottentot who's never heard of Christ have to go down to hell automatically just because she or he wasn't sprinkled with a few drops of consecrated holy water? God wouldn't be so cruel as to demand that. Still, Hottentots might be safe if their religion, whatever it is, doesn't have a concept of hell. Indian gurus are pretty safe. Their concept of hell is coming back here to a dreary life. Seems like only Christians have problems with going to hell. Maybe that's why I'm a Rationalist Christian. Rationalist Christians don't believe in hell.

When I asked Julie and Glen why they didn't marry they just looked at each other and didn't say anything. Then I remembered that time when Julie came to see me. She told me she did want to marry Glen. But she didn't feel it was right to ask him to be committed to someone with a disability. I told her that if you have a child together you are committed and that's all there is to it. Julie could see that. One advantage of being blind is that you can see lots of things.

You ask me who I am and I'll tell you. I'm a matriarch and I have strong ideas.

In 1945 my dear husband came back from the war. He was no longer the enthusiastic, naive Cain who had left me those long years ago. When I saw him at the wharf it was such a strange meeting. I'd left the children with the neighbours, told my family not to come and gone alone. When he came down the gangway I wasn't sure if it was him at all. He looked at me with a frightened question mark in his eyes. Should I embrace this man? Would I foolishly make a show of affection for someone I did not know? But it was Cain. He held me limply in his arms while I tried to think of something to say. Not the old Cain. Somehow that innocence had been ground into the dust and blood of the battlefield. On that first day home we sat in the kitchen. The children had greeted the stranger with a singular lack of concern and run out into the garden to play.

"My father's come back from the war," cried Luke.

"He's my father too," said Anne possessively. She had been just a baby when he left and had no idea of what the concept of having a father meant.

He was still in uniform. He'd laid his khaki kitbag against the wall with his lemon-squeezer hat on top. I had poured a cup of tea.

"It's strange to drink out of china," he said.

"I suppose it must be."

"Tin cups and mess tins. They're still in my kit."

He looked around the familiar kitchen, which still badly needed a coat of paint. I couldn't think of anything to say. What was he doing here? Where had he come from? I hadn't seen this man before. What right had he to come here and sit in my kitchen?

"You'll have to get used to mufti," I said at last.

"Mufti..." He didn't seem to hear. "I thought I was with God when I was in the desert."

"Did you dear?"

"The nights were very cold...." He put his cup down in the saucer and gazed at some point in the far distance. Silence in the room, just the tick tock of the clock.

"What happened?"

"In the desert. The nights were very cold. I thought about you."

There was nothing I could think of to reply to that.

"It's Mother's birthday on Sunday."

"Oh?" He seemed surprised that Mother should actually exist.

"We're going for Sunday dinner, after church. Nothing special is planned. I usually help Mother with the roast beforehand. Will you come?"

He didn't answer that question, but he seemed to brighten. "They didn't come to the boat...."

"I asked them not to."

"Not to? I would have liked to have seen them."

"Robbie will be there too."

"Oh? You know you never mentioned him in your letters. Where has he been?"

"He's just got out of jail."

"Jail?"

"He organised a lag for himself. He thought it would be better to be safe and sound in jail than to be killed in a war."

"Would Robbie say that?"

"It's what he thought."

"I'm tired. I'd like to take a nap."

Cain lay down on our big bed and slept and slept. At bedtime I woke him. He undressed like a zombie, still asleep. I crept under the covers and lay down beside the snoring hulk, beside the strange smell of the man that I had missed for so long. He awoke in the early hours of the morning and we made love. A strange clumsy reunion after being apart for so long. Before we could talk he turned over and fell asleep again. A little later he awoke and we remembered some of the little secret things we had done together in the past. I thought that might be the home-coming, but he was asleep again.

"Is that man still here," asked Anne at breakfast.

"He's your daddy," I told her.

"Where's he going to sleep?"

"In the big bed. With me."

"Does that mean I can't come in?"

Cain was always a stranger to his children. They had relied on me for so long and nothing could change that. In time he returned somewhat to his old self, but for me there was always a shadow. He had been taken by the war and had never returned.

I always went to the manse on Sunday mornings to help Mother with the roast. She didn't seem to be able to manage by herself. Housework was undertaken by Father somehow, with the assistance of some ladies of the congregation. Mother had become fragile, as though she was about to take her first step into heaven. She no longer fretted and worried as she had before, but she was, how can I say it? Distant? It seemed that she was living in some faraway magical world, a bourn which none of us mundane beings were permitted to enter. The only part of the real world that had any meaning for her was the garden. Occasionally she would look at you with a gleam of knowledge in her eye and then make a mysterious comment that seemed very profound. When you thought about it, it made sense in a peculiar way, but as though it were in a language for which no-one possessed a Rosetta stone. People do make profound comments when they are drunk or drugged. If you are sober when in the company of intoxicated people their thoughts don't seem so profound at all. It was different with Mother. You knew that what she said had a special meaning to herself and no-one else.

When I arrived the roast had been placed in the oven by Father at Mother's Special Temperature. It was my duty to peel the vegetables and place them on the roasting tray at The Right Time and at Mother's Special Going To Church Temperature. These Temperatures had been carefully recorded in the back of the Edmonds Cookery Book. Also peas were podded or beans cut and placed in a pot of salted water for cooking later. The presence of an Atlas Electric Range in the manse made the preparation of Sunday roast easy. In the old days Mother had managed it with a wood range. Now that was a work of art.

When Mother saw Cain her face brightened with recognition. He was wearing his uniform and campaign ribbons. "Why did you go away for so long? We've missed you." She touched Cain's cheek with her palm. "Fighting in the war? Such a long time. You did good work. The Lord's work. Evil was defeated. Are you coming to church with us?"

"Of course."

"The sheep that was lost has been found. See it lying in the manger."

"Um, the Bishop is coming for dinner," said Father quickly. "I invited him. Oh well I suppose he invited himself."

"What Bishop is this?" I asked.

"Our Bishop. Bishop Slender. He visits the churches in the diocese as often as he can."

This visit from the Bishop concerned me. Father had been preaching somewhat radical sermons in recent times and there was an undercurrent of disapproval among certain conservative members of the congregation which, I am sure, had trickled back to chancery.

The Bishop was waiting outside the church when we arrived. He was a plump man with a round face and small eyes. He was dressed in a business suit with a purple shirt and clerical collar. One of those men of the Church who put their career before Love of God I thought uncharitably. For a moment I thought he was going to sit with us but no.

"I'll sit in the back pew if you don't mind. I like to see how many parishioners fall asleep during the service. Ha ha. The acid test of a good sermon"

"That's all right," said Father. "I've chosen The Epistle to the Ephesians, verses five, for my text.

"Most appropriate. Ha ha. Most appropriate."

I had the feeling that Bishop Slender could not place this particular verse. Father read it during the sermon.

"Awake thou that sleepest,
and arise from the dead,
and Christ shall give thee light."

During the Parish announcements Father made a point of welcoming Cain home. He also introduced the Bishop and informed the congregation that if any of them fell asleep during the sermon his head would be on the block.

After the service many of the congregation came to talk to Cain. It was Mrs Smithers, the plump, bustling war widow who arranged a welcome home afternoon tea party. Cain merely said that he didn't consider himself a hero or worth the fuss. Nevertheless we agreed to come.

When we arrived home for mid-day dinner Robbie was there, looking very sharp but prison pale. The Bishop barely seemed to acknowledge his existence when introduced. Just a limp touch of the hand. I imagine he was aware of the criminal record.

"A glass of sherry before the meal, Vicar?" asked the Bishop.

"Only port I'm afraid. I keep it for distraught parishioners."

The two of them went into Father's study. I don't know what they talked about. Pleasantries before the meal I imagine. One never discussed serious business before a meal. There was a discussion afterwards though. Cain told me all about that.

The Bishop said Grace: "We thank thee O Lord for the bounty of this table and pray to the light that thy bright spirit descend and honour us with thy ineffable grace. Amen."

I wondered where he'd got that one from. Father offered the Bishop the dignity of carving the roast, while I supervised the vegetables. All the food was placed on plates or in bowls on the table and you helped yourself.

"Do you like peas, Bishop Slim?" asked Mother.

"Yes. Very much."

"They were picked from our garden. Matthew grew them. He's not much of a gardener you know, but I make him do it."

The Bishop looked at Father. There was a question in his eyes. Why had he been called 'Slim'? Father turned to the children and began cutting up their food.

"A piece of lamb, Mrs Tunnicliffe?" asked the Bishop.

"A small portion if you don't mind. I have to watch my weight." The Bishop passed her a piece. Mother had placed small portions on her plate, as she usually did. "It's cooked with rosemary you know. Does Mrs Slim use rosemary?"

"Ah, Slender. Ah, no I believe not."

"Mrs Kuzimich told me about it. It's a Dalmatian idea. Rosemary, that's for remembrance."

"Ah, indeed." The Bishop heaped generous helpings of food onto his plate and smothered them with gravy and mint sauce. He was out of his depth with Mother.

"And rue you know, that's for sorrow. We don't use rue in this household."

"Ha, ha. Millicent played Ophelia in Hamlet you know," said Father.

"Yes I did dear. For our local Rep, when I was in England," replied Mother.

"Ah yes, very talented," said the Bishop. "You play the violin I believe?"

But Mother cut him off.

"She was mad you know. She drowned in a brook among plants with obscene names. They were the herbs of her destiny. And all she wanted to do was love poor Hamlet. But he hated women. He thought they were breeders of sinners."

There was silence around the table.

"Mummy, can I have a drink?" asked Luke.

Father went into the kitchen for a glass of milk. "I'll be growing Brussels sprouts in the winter," he said when he returned.

Mother pecked at her peas with the fork. Conversation resumed.

After the meal the Bishop suggested that the men go into the study for brandy. Cigars weren't mentioned, but then nobody smoked. The Bishop had brought a small squat bottle with him and father managed to find glasses in the china cabinet. The Bishop seemed to think it civilized to have brandy after a meal. I could guess that it was his regular custom.

Mother and I walked in the garden. The children had been put in old pinnies that Mother kept for these occasions, and sent to the sand pit to play.

"Matthew can't leave his church," said Mother. "He'd be lost if he didn't have anywhere to preach."

"I don't see how he's going to leave the church."

"The Bishop has plans." Mother stopped by her yellow rose and inspected the leaves. "Too many aphids. It's been a wet season." She shook the leaf. "He's an avocado."

"What?"

"Advocate. For the Devil. You get it everywhere, even in the church. He was born in a manger wasn't He?"

"What are you talking about Mother."

"Matthew. He means well but I don't understand why he wants to change the story of baby Jesus. Bishop Slimley doesn't like it. You can see it in his eyes."

"Father is a liberal preacher. Just because he doesn't believe in the Gospel stories of the nativity doesn't mean he's not a True Christian."

"The church doesn't like it. It's not what they preach."

"The church is an old fogey. Is that the reason for this Bishop's visit. Is he checking up on Father?"

Mother looked distracted. She had brought her shears and snipped a flower from the white camellia. The petals had gone brown at the edges. "Will you put this in the compost for me dear? I forgot to bring my gloves. Rust and moth doth corrupt. Flowers grow pure white in heaven."

She gave me the flower and wandered down the path. When we returned to the house, via the compost heap, Robbie was sitting at the table fuming.

"What's the matter dear?" asked Mother.

"The Bishop didn't like my jokes."

"But he's a Christian Bishop, dear. He'll laugh at an ecclesiastical joke."

"I wanted to tell him the one about the Pope and the actress."

"He'd enjoy a joke about the Pope, but not one about an actress."

I couldn't understand Mother. When talking to Robbie she suddenly seemed alive, back in the real world.

"Nothing would get a smile out of him."

"I saw him smile at the table, when we talked about poverty. Let me lean on your arm. I'll show you the lilies in the garden. They weave not, neither do they spin."

Cain told me later what had transpired in the study. First the Bishop poured a measure of brandy into each bowl, sniffed his portion and sipped with a secret smile of satisfaction.

"We didn't have time for secret sniffs of satisfaction in the war," Cain told me.

Then, apropos of nothing, he related disreputable stories about drinking during the war. In the desert he'd become friendly with Tom, an MO. Tom had a friend in Supplies and hence he was able to obtain quantities of medicinal alcohol. It was required for sterilisation of equipment Cain told me, although I don't know whether that is true or not. Anyway they'd mix the alcohol with orange juice fifty/fifty in a jug put out by Walt Disney. This jug was moulded in the shape of Donald Duck. Tom and Cain and a couple of their mates would sit in the back of an ambulance getting intoxicated on this concoction. They called it 'duck's piss'.

In Italy, he said, they had a big pit dug in the ground and they'd rage around all night in the bottom of it drinking the local wine. It was purple Ruffino he said. And was it Ruffino!? There was no time for a secret sniff of satisfaction in the war. The booze tasted awful. It was an anaesthetic which kept you going in a world of carnage and destruction. Perhaps the army were aware of this use for medicinal alcohol.

"The Bishop was in control of the conversation," said Cain. "Very adroit in manipulating its direction. He became a Bishop because of this ability to manipulate, and, I imagine, impress the right people, not because of piety. He started out by relating titbits of news from the diocese. His personal assistant had been transferred. This meant the assistant personal assistant had to be promoted to take his place, leaving a vacancy further down the line."

"Is this hinting at what I think it is?" I asked.

"He seemed to be telling Matthew that there'd always be a job for him in chancery."

"The church always takes care of its own," said the Bishop.

"Looks like I might want to apply for a job there eh Bishop," said Robbie. He was annoyed. He had been allocated a bowl of brandy but, apart from that, the Bishop was not acknowledging his presence.

"Do you have any qualifications?" asked the Bishop.

"Son of a Vicar. Brought up in a Christian family. I knock around a lot with sinners, just like His Nibs used to do."

"Then what sort of work activity are you qualified to undertake?"

"I hardly think Robbie's serious," put in Father.

"Let him speak for himself Vicar. Robbie?"

"I can show you a trick with seventy-one cards."

"Ha ha. Hardly appropriate. Ha ha. You must have something you can tell us."

"There's the story about the Pope and the actress."

"Robbie, there's no need for this," said Father.

"You might prefer the one about the Bishop and the Hottentot."

Robbie was being his charming best. Cain told me that he could hardly stop himself from laughing. I didn't think it was very funny. Robbie was just making it more difficult for Father. The Bishop's cheeks flushed to a deeper shade of their normal ruddy be-veined purple.

"Robbie, this is not necessary," said Father.

"Sorry. I'm really not used to high-class company. Excuse me please." Robbie drained his bowl and left.

"I'm sorry," said Father.

"The lamb has strayed," replied the Bishop, taking a sip of brandy. "The Good Shepherd must seek and find."

"Then it was our turn," Cain told me. "Yours and mine. I got somewhat annoyed with the Bishop. I guess I lost my senses."

My poor dear innocent and honest Cain. He was always losing his senses. I sometimes wish I could afford to do so myself.

The Bishop began to ask questions. "You've just returned home I believe?"

"Yes," replied Cain.

"There is a time to adjust to civilian life. Where were you posted?"

"In the desert. Tobruk. Then Italy."

"Ah. A seasoned campaigner. What will you be doing now that you're back in mufti?"

"Oh resurrect the family business." Cain thought for one terrible moment that the Bishop was thinking of offering him that job in chancery.

"You actually kept a business going during the war?"

"Old Smithers looked after it, and my wife did the accounts."

"Thriving is it?"

"Just a bookshop. Dreamers Bookshop."

"Dreamers? But you specialise in free-thinking literature. At least that's what I've been lead to believe."

"We have a Rationalist side and a Christian side. My father established the Rationalist content. When I became a Christian I initiated the religious side."

"Your father. Not Montague Abel?"

"Yes, that was my father."

"I read his books. I wished to test myself, just as the Lord was tested in the wilderness. Fortunately I was immune to temptation."

"Oh Montague had a lot of good points," put in Father who had been sitting in silence, wondering what this conversation was all about. "In fact I agreed with many of them."

"If you call blasphemy a good point. You can't agree with blasphemy."

"I imagine blasphemy doesn't mean much to someone who isn't a Christian," said Father.

"That may be so. But you invited his son into your house."

"And converted him to Christianity also," Cain blurted out in anger. "My father and I were both welcome in his house. Matthew taught me that Christ associated with sinners. Does the church teach now that you should not?"

The Bishop did not answer for a moment. He was adroit at handling situations like this. "No, of course not. The church teaches us to be compassionate. All stray sheep are welcome back into the fold. I am impressed, Vicar, that you should save one who was so surely led astray."

Cain told me that he was not impressed by this patronising pomposity. He strongly disliked being called a sheep. I mean who'd want to be? They are the most stupid animal you'd ever meet. He almost thought of telling the Bishop that I was a Rationalist but decided against it.

"I can make my own decisions, Bishop Sallow. I don't have to be led this way or that." Cain was getting mighty annoyed.

"Indeed."

"You can say that Christ drew me into the fold. All Matthew did was point me in the direction of the light."

"Everything you know is what Matthew taught you?"

"No, he just opened my eyes. My father was a professional Rationalist. Matthew is a better Rationalist than he ever was, and yet he's a Christian."

"Indeed."

At that point there was a knock on the door. It was Luke to tell his Daddy that he wanted to go home. I'd sent him because I'd heard the pitch of Cain's voice.

It was later in the evening, when Cain and I were putting the children to bed, that I received the phone call.

"Millicent has died," said Father. "She's at peace at last."

The second rose of remembrance that I planted in my garden was the Apocathory's Rose, the red rose of Lancaster. The white rose of York, for Montague, grows close by in a gesture of reconciliation between the Rationalist and the Christian.

9

Things changed for Father after Mother died. The Bishop conducted the funeral service and gave unctuous words of comfort for the bereaved family. He offered Father a locum for a few weeks. Father did not accept, saying he needed to keep himself busy as the best way of coping with his grief. The congregation came around in support and withdrew their previous complaints. You see now why things had changed. Ministers of Religion are required to present a perfect face to the world. They are doors to the Kingdom of God, where all is pure and serene. If a flaw enters into the world of a Minister then the door to that perfect peace is seen to have closed. Mother's illness was perceived as a flaw, the work of a demon. It was Father's duty to cast out demons, as Christ did, but he could not do so. In the end death cast out the demon and laid it to rest.

The Bishop departed. He died soon after, having choked on the crumb of a muffin that he had attempted to swill down with a glass of brandy.

It was Mother that saved Father. She died to save him.

Now, who else came to see me yesterday? Oh yes, Anne's two children, Tracy and Glen. Tracy is twenty-four and still flits around from trendy boyfriend to trendy patisserie in her modern way. When I was her age I was married and settled down. Well no, not really settled if I remember correctly, the children weren't born then and I was trying to be modern myself, disagreeing with everything and all that. Being modern in those days was different to what it is now. What was considered modern when I was young is considered old-fashioned now, and so it goes on through the generations. I think it was Plato who called the young generation of his time a pack of long-haired louts. History always repeats itself.

They're good grandchildren though. I know they'd rather be out dining and going to cocktail parties than paying their duty by coming to visit this decrepit old body, but they still make the effort to come. I can't imagine why Anne and Charles wanted to call them Tracy and Glen, I mean what sort of names are those? I remember having quite a row when they chose them, all to no avail.

"Just let me do something I want to for once, Mum. They're my children."

I never stopped her from doing what she wanted to, unless it was dangerous or bad for her health. I suppose I shouldn't have brought it up.

None of my business really. You know how touchy new mothers are. Charles looked at me as though I was the interfering mother-in-law and gave me the cold shoulder. I respect him for that. Standing up for his wife the way he should.

I seem to be thinking of all the times in my life where there were troubles, arguments, disputes of some kind. It's by disputes that you learn and reach a resolution to a problem where before there was only ignorance. I never was an argumentative person, not really. Strong willed maybe. I only argued if I thought it was important, a matter of principle. You can enjoy a good argument, but you can't enjoy a row. No, the only times that remain in my mind are the occasions where I was in the wrong. Arguments with my family... with religion... they say you should never argue about religion... at least I'm not arguing about politics.

I dream about the days that were important, about the things that have to be put right. But how do you set them right? Say you are sorry? Take responsibility for what you have done? Time is short now and we would like to look forward to a happy ending. Or would we? Dying is not a happy ending, but then it is the end to all stories. Once the bad guys have been defeated and the hero and heroine ride off into the sunset there is still the next day to live through... and the day after that... until the last...

When I was young, there was love and romance, butterfly cakes and lemonade in the summerhouse. But I always knew that the perfect petals of the rose would one day turn brown and wither and fall away. All things develop and grow until they reach the prime of perfection and then there follows a strange, slow dissolution. What was beautiful becomes changed, ugly, perverted, rotten, a gnarled husk to be cast back into the earth from which it came. But even so that brings renewal.

A friend of mine, Janine, was fit and healthy until the day she died. She was at the supermarket and had a dizzy fit. She sat down on the shop floor and went out... like a light. That's the way it should be, not with suffering. If there is joy at the start of life why should there be pain at the end?

Cain never talked much about his religious beliefs, except once he said he heard a small voice... a small voice in the middle of a storm... he wondered why I couldn't hear it. I was sure that I never did. Although perhaps there was one fine day when I was a child and Ugly Jesus spoke to my fingers... But that's a silly fancy. I've gone into the subject of religion quite carefully. Studied it with the rational mind. I didn't see a lot of what might make sense. I didn't hear any small voice crying above the storm. I tell you, I've been honest about it all, you can't damn me for that.

I've led a good life. I would say my deeds merit reward, not punishment, so if there is a God who's going to punish me for not going through some dull ritual in a church then He is not much of a God. Evil people always draw pain in on themselves. I've noticed that in life. People who are fabulously wealthy are never happy if the whole of their attention is centred on their selfish wealth and power. I think it's called the law of karma or something except there are cases where fine people suffer afflictions. Now there's a mystery. You have to go into past lives to solve that one. That's what the Hindu gurus say.

Cain and I had to avoid discussing our beliefs because each of us felt so strongly about them. Well if he's right we'll meet up in heaven, but if he's not who knows...

Cain and I had an idyllic relationship until he went away to the war. The problem was that he never really came back to me. Not the same man. A part of him remained behind in the desert, under the cold light of the stars. He was bemused by the world of death and destruction that took his innocence and gave nothing in return. It was then that I learnt the meaning of the phrase, 'man of straw'. He went through his life like an automaton, changing the gears without any thought of joy or involvement. He ran the business, tolerably well but without enthusiasm. We got by on the income. He went to church and sang hymns as before, but sometimes I saw him looking furtively up to the ceiling, as though he wanted to catch the eye of God. And he always remained a stranger to his children. They looked upon him as though he were merely a friend of the family, who was somehow allowed to sleep in the same bed as Mummy.

"We shouldn't have more children," he said one day. "It wouldn't be fair on the ones we have."

Thereafter we took 'precautions' on the occasions that we made love.

As the years went by he started to age, much more quickly that he should. As though his body was saying - 'let's get it over and done with.' In the end the canker of the mind became a malignant infestation of the body. The doctors called it cancer and took him to hospital. When there was nothing more they could do they sent him back to me to die. A stick man who had to be fed and washed and clothed. It was school holidays and I sent the children away to camp. I wondered if they would see him again.

Cain came back to me finally, for a brief moment before the light went out. That is a moment to treasure, to hold in your heart forever. I had asked Father to come and give Communion.

"Will you take it with me?" asked Cain.

"Of course."

I held his hand and stroked his brow. His body was just a wasted skeleton but a light came into his eyes.

"You don't believe in it."

"Yes I do." I had to give him solace. "I've always believed in Communion."

"Matthew's a better Rationalist than you are." His voice was a grating whisper.

"Don't talk, you'll tire yourself."

He sat up on his pillow. Drew himself up. Somehow I sensed the old Cain had returned.

"Something I want to tell you."

"What?"

"I haven't been much good since I came back from the war."

"No."

"I thought I was with God when I was in the desert. The nights were cold. So clear. You could look up and see heaven in the stars. Made me think of the forty days and forty nights when Christ fasted in the wilderness. One night, when I was on guard, a shell came..." He let go of my hand and gazed at some point in the far distance. Silence in the room, vague noises from the world outside.

"What happened?"

"My mates, who were in our tent, they copped it. I was away at the perimeter. Two dead, one died in hospital. The others were patched up and sent home. If it wasn't my turn for guard duty I'd have been in there with them... They weren't heroes, they weren't out in the battlefield fighting for their country, they were just asleep. One chance in a million. I thought God must have been with me. I couldn't understand why He wasn't in the tent with them. I told the Padre. He didn't have any answers."

"What answers?"

"I had to question the goodness of God. The use of anything. There weren't any answers. I came back from the war and went through the old rituals without wanting to be involved. I didn't know if I believed in anything. All I ever thought was I wanted to be back there with them."

"In the tent?"

"I thought it was meant to be."

I got angry with him. "No you weren't meant to be killed in a tent. You were meant to be here with me. Now I'm telling you."

"You're right. I should have come back to you. I'm sorry."

He lay back on the pillow. Exhausted. Peace in his eyes. The storm-tossed vessel home to a safe haven. I could only think of pleasantries.

"Robbie's coming to Communion too. Father said they had good news."

"Good news?"

"About Robbie. At least he's stopped offending."

"Yes." He looked at me. "Something I wanted to say..."

"What?"

"I love you."

"I know."

I stayed there with him. He fell asleep after a while.

Cain and I had our day of love and romance under the golden light of the sun and under the gelid light of the moon. In spite of whatever abundance there is in the moment we know that in the end a cold wind will blow up from the ice, bringing winter to the landscape of the heart. And when you look to the eye of the sun what do you find? Light, or dark.? There's a dark side to the sun. It is a side you never see.

I went into the kitchen, sat at the table and wept. There was no fathom to the abyss of my grief. I'd recovered by the time Father and Robbie arrived. Matthew sat on the chair beside me, looked at my red eyes, put his hand on my arm.

"How is he?"

"Asleep."

"He wanted Communion. We'll give him a few minutes."

"Father...?"

"Yes."

"Can I join you... for Communion."

He looked at me with a question in his eye. "Of course."

Robbie was standing by the stove. He looked cold. Prison grey, although he'd been out for months. He had that shifty look I knew well. He'd been up to something.

"You had some news you said?" I asked Father.

He brightened, drew himself up. "Let's wait until we're with Cain."

We sat for quarter of an hour making small talk. Robbie was mostly silent. Eventually I looked in on Cain, wiped his forehead, and he awoke. We brought chairs from the kitchen, sat around the bed.

"Ah Cain, good to see you home at last." Father had a small case containing the paraphernalia for the service.

Robbie shook Cain's hand. I couldn't understand why but a bond had been developing between them since Cain became ill.

"Nice to see you Robbie," he said.

"Good to see you mate," said Robbie. "Give that old worm the heave ho eh."

"Not much chance of that."

Matthew moved the small table by the window to beside the bed. "Our Communion table. Well Robbie and I have excellent news. You tell them Robbie."

Robbie looked at me, guilt in his eyes. "I have been accepted for the ministry."

Matthew took his son's hand. "You see, the prodigal has returned, and made good. Oh we had to work hard to achieve it, but we did it. We had to work and pray and in the end the Lord was willing."

"I always thought you would do it," said Cain "We must kill the fatted calf."

"All in good time. All in good time. I might sit for a moment." Father sat on the visitors chair. He looked tired, exhausted.

"Are you all right Matthew?' asked Cain.

"The excitement gets to you. And the infirmities of age." He looked around, somehow lost. "I may be passing the parish on... to a younger man."

"You're not old Father," I told him.

"You still have work to complete," said Cain.

"Perhaps." Father took a bottle of French Champagne from his case and placed it on the table. "I thought we might have something a little better than communion wine. Lucy dear, do you have glasses? Don't worry, it's been properly sanctified. I've chilled it too. Robbie, you can pop the cork." I fetched glasses, Robbie popped and poured. Father stood, prayer book in hand. "No sipping now. Wait for the service."

We started with the Lords Prayer. I knelt beside the bed and held Cain's hand. He clung to me as though he was trying to will God to come to me through him.

Father prayed: "*ALMIGHTY God, unto whom all hearts be open, all desires known, and from whom no secrets are hid... through Christ our Lord. Amen.*"

We opened our eyes, looked up

"Our Lord Jesus Christ said: Hear, O Israel, ... Thou shalt love the Lord thy God with all thy heart, with all thy soul, with all thy mind, and with all thy strength...."

I found myself mumbling the response with the others

"Lord have mercy upon us, and incline our hearts to keep this law."

Father's voice took on a timbre, a passion of beauty, uttering words of power. Words that moved me although I could not accept their meaning.

"I BELIEVE in one God the Father Almighty, Maker of heaven and earth.." And on and on. *"Amen."*

"Amen." We echoed.

"Let us pray for the whole state of Christ's Church militant here in earth..."

The words of the prayer to the Queen and council washed over me like so many waves on the beach. Then followed the request for repentance.

"YE that do truly and earnestly repent you of your sins... and intend to lead a new life, following the commandments of God...."

I remembered these past years with Cain when I sinned by the sin of omission, of denying him my complete understanding, by blaming him and the war for the distance in our relationship. I never though to repent for the animosity I'd felt towards Robbie. Not at that time. There he was kneeling beside me pretending, I thought, to enumerate the catalogue of his cast of evil. I hoped he saw the vision in his mind of a despicable act to a violin case.

"ALMIGHTY God, Father of our Lord Jesus Christ, Maker of all things, Judge of all men; We acknowledge and bewail our manifold sins and wickedness... We do earnestly repent..."

We mumbled the responses, reading from the prayer book. *"ALMIGHTY God, our heavenly Father... Have mercy upon you; pardon and deliver you from all your sins... Amen."*

"Lift up your hearts," intoned Father.

"We lift them up unto the Lord," we responded.

"Let us give thanks unto our Lord God."

"It is meet and right so to do."

"Holy, holy, holy, Lord God of hosts, heaven and earth are full of thy glory: Glory be to thee, O Lord most High. Amen."

Then more prayers and the delivery of the Communion.

"We are not worthy so much as to gather up the crumbs under thy table..."

Then the Communion. First the bread.

"The Body of our Lord Jesus Christ... Take and eat this in remembrance that Christ died for thee, and feed on him in thy heart by faith with thanksgiving."

Father then held my glass of wine high and smiled. It seemed to me it was not a glass but a copper-wrought chalice, old and dented in the upper room of a house in a hilltop village, so long ago. Robbie took my hand and Father took his, while he continued with the service. Here we were together as a family, worshipping Christ as we had so many years ago. Following the ritual we had followed so many times on Sunday mornings in the peaceful holiness of the church.

"OUR Father, which art in heaven..."

"...the most precious Body and Blood of thy Son our Saviour Jesus Christ..."

The service ended. The spell was broken.

"Thank you for that Lucy," said Cain.

I did not know how to reply. I looked at Cain. Looked in his eyes, and then I knew we were together again. And he was a Christian, and I was a Rationalist, and that was all right.

I turned and looked at Robbie. He was standing there with the light of heaven in his eyes. The renewed man who had most certainly had Communion with God. How could he do that? How could he be such a charlatan? And how could Father be taken in with such a theatrical performance.

"Cain and I would like to have a chat, if that is all right," said Father. "And we have a glass of champagne to share."

"I shall go to the kitchen and knock up a batch of pikelets." I said.

"Pikelets. That sounds nice," said Father.

Robbie and I were in the kitchen. Robbie sitting in the kitchen chair. I was sifting flour, baking powder, salt into a bowl.

"A cup of coffee would be nice." said Robbie.

"There's instant in the cupboard." I wasn't going to drop everything and make him a cup of coffee.'"We're a tea household anyway."

"Tea then."

"When they've finished."

"Alright Sister, when they've finished."

I took another bowl from the shelf and began to beat an egg and the sugar.

"Why are you becoming a minister?" I asked.

"Because I've seen the error of me ways."

"I don't believe that."

"Gospel truth. I've seen the light. I know the way. All has been made straight."

"Pig's bum."

"Can I show you the five card trick?" He took a pack of cards from his pocket.

"Put them away. I'm not interested in cards."

"It's my Bible. You know the story about the soldier who played cards in church?"

"I've heard the song." There was a popular song, monologue, about a soldier in the war, caught playing cards in church, who made up some story about how they were a Bible and Prayer book.

"Don't you trust me?"

"You're good for a laugh at times."

"Good for a laugh..."

"Why should I be fond of you. You think you have an amusing personality. But it's your refusal to be honest that I find frivolous."

"I am as pure as the driven snow."

"Oh don't be so stupid." Suddenly it came upon me. The grief that I had been holding inside. Grief for Cain and his dying. Grief for the many years we had been apart. I just stood there and cried, and salt tears trickled down my cheeks.

"What's the matter Sis?" I heard Robbie's voice coming from a distance.

"Are you so self-centred you can't see it?"

"Cain?"

"What else."

"I'm sorry Sis."

"He asked for Communion because he thinks he's going to die."

"He is going to die Lucy."

Of course he was going to die. I knew he was going to die. I could not accept that such a thing was going to happen. I had a tremendous argument with God for letting such a thing happen. I had a tremendous argument with Robbie for pretending to want to be a Minister of Faith. I could say nothing except: "I'm sorry. It's not a peaceful day."

"No" Robbie put his arm around me. Something I had to accept. Felt comforted to have someone holding me at that time. "He's not going out just yet."

"No. A week... or two."

"You have that time."

"That time. What time?"

Knowing also that there was to be an end soon, I stopped weeping. I added milk and the dry ingredients to the beaten egg and sugar and began stirring.

"There's not much time for me either. I've only really started getting on well with Cain quite recently. More to him than I thought."

I didn't want to talk about Cain to Robbie. There was something more important to discuss. "Now you have to tell me why you have taken to the ministry?"

"I'm committed to Christ."

"Bullshit."

"Well you never know, there could be something in it."

"Something to it? Yes Robbie, that's you. You're in this for your own advantage. You always hated the church."

"Oh no, I enjoyed the time when I put the frog in the baptismal font."

"Yes, it was you."

"Of course." Robbie was gloating. "And I liked some of the sermons. Do you remember the time he said the nativity stories were a myth?"

"He said they were a symbol of truth."

"Something like that."

"And the one where he said that Jesus was ugly?"

"Well what's wrong with that. It wouldn't make any change to Christianity if he was."

"Ah, and here's a Rationalist talking. The congregation doesn't always take kindly to these ideas."

"Well he preaches liberal views to a pack of fundamentalists. He's always done it."

"They're starting to mutter again. I don't think he's well either."

"What do you mean?"

"He says it's a twinge. I don't know. He wants me to take over."

"I see. And preach to the congregation on the many ways of extracting money from helpless widows."

"It's all right Sister. I don't want to take over his church. I want to deal with the crims. At least I have some expertise..."

I greased my large frying-pan with butter and put it on the gas.

"Well just tell me exactly what you are up to." I was angry with him. I had to keep an eye on that frying-pan. It always heated up quickly.

"It's a job I could do."

"I don't know what you mean. You don't even believe in it. How could you be a minister?"

Robbie had started pacing about the room. He had his back to me, looking at fly spots on the wall. "What other job am I going to get with a record like mine? Shovelling shit is about all I'd ever get. I've got a wife and a kid. Molly stuck by me through most of it. I owe her something."

"So you intend to become a minister of the church so you can have a job?"

"If you want to put it like that."

"I think you're disgusting."

"For God's sake Lucy, you never give me a chance. I need a job. I can't just lag around for the rest of my life. I took things from people. Now I owe. I've changed. I want to make up for it."

I could almost hear the violins playing in the background. I spooned pikelet mixture into the frying pan and turned down the gas.

"Oh my brilliant brother, he wants to make up for a life of sin. So you con your father... And after all the things you did to Mother."

"Things? What things?"

"Distressing her the way you did, by being in jail."

"Don't blame me for Mother's illness."

"She should have had the operation."

"She would have been a vegetable..."

"She suffered anguish."

"She might have suffered, but she was still in the world."

"You were never there."

"I was with her on the last day. I'd just come out of my final lag. We walked in the garden. She was perfectly normal. Told me all about the flowers. She told me the garden was choked out with tares. She said the whole world was full of them but one day a gardener would come and remove them. The garden didn't seem to be neglected to me. There were some nice flowers growing in it. She gave me one of those lilies from under the hedge. She knew she was going to die that day so she gave me the flower. They smother you in lilies when you die, they have the sweet smell of death. Then she thanked me for the years I had given her on earth."

"Just a walk in the garden. Does that mean anything?" Somehow the words Robbie said moved me. I could believe that he was being honest for one time in his life.

112

"She walked all her life in a garden, it became full of weeds but then she found a flower."

"Yes. A flower."

"She picked another lily and she said: 'If I give this lily to the Bishop do you think he will leave us alone?' Do you know what she meant?" I looked at him. I did not know what to say. "No-one has greater love than this..." He was misquoting from the Gospel of John.

It's the people that write these tragedies. They write down the pages in their own blood. It's not caused by some God up in heaven looking down on us and pulling our marionette strings.

"I don't know." I just couldn't say anything sensible.

"Is that something burning?"

I looked at the pikelets. I'd forgotten about them. They'd burnt to a crisp. I scraped them into the rubbish and put the fry pan under the tap.

"That's the end of that." I said.

It was then that Father came into the room. So old, so tired, so quiet. You would have thought he was a mouse. I looked into his eyes and I saw death, and I knew instantly what had happened.

"Lucy?"

"Yes Father?"

"Yes. It's Cain."

"I know." It was a dream. It was not happening to me. The world was numb, cold, ethereal..

"He's gone," said Father with finality.

"Gone."

"After Communion we sat down with the champagne. He told me... made his confession.... he seemed to be at peace... then, he just slipped... slipped away."

"He can't go. At least he could have given me a couple of weeks."

"It's all right Lucy, it's all right." Father put his arms around me.

"It's all right Sister, it's all right." Robbie put his arms around us both.

"He had no right to go."

"It's all right Lucy, it's all right."

"It's all right Sister."

"It's not all right. It's not all right. It's not, all right."

There was pikelet mixture still in the bowl but now it would never be eaten.

10

I think there's a light at the window. Just the faint rosy glimmer before dawn. I look forward to the daytime. It is when the dark becomes light that we are able to see things as they are. When I go it will have to be in the light, then I could wave good-bye to all the dark things in my life. Then I can leave them behind.

I planted a white rose for the memory of Cain. It's name is 'Innocence'. A single white tea rose with red and gold in the centre. The white of the petals is for purity of the soul. The red in the centre is remembrance of the blood of his friends who died on the battlefield. And the gold? That is for richness of spirit. It grows between the roses of York and Lancaster that I planted for Mother and Montague. I placed it there in the expectation that it might help to reconcile those two tempestuous lives. That if they met in heaven, or wherever they might meet, they would be friends

There never was a finer man that walked the face of the earth. We had lost each other for a time, then on the day when we found ourselves he was taken from me. We should have had more time together. There never was a finer Christian man...

I wondered, in my dark times, if I should blame someone, something for taking him from me. Should one blame God? Or should one forgive God?

I sometimes thought I should blame God. Then I remembered a person I had known who said she no longer believed in God because her son died a terrible death. Cancer. She was punishing God for causing this death, by withholding her belief. As if He was directly responsible. Now that's a good punishment for God. Don't believe in Him and He might go away and not cause people to die from cancer. As if God existed purely because of people's belief.

But can you blame God for the tragedies in our lives? That is a question. I believe that if there is a God, He is detached, not involved in the everyday affairs of mice and... and people. God allows the winds of chance to blow, and they blow where they will. I do not accept the hoary concept that God is an old man with a white beard sitting up in heaven on a golden throne, looking down on Earth and controlling the doings of men. We'd all be puppets without a thought in our head.

But it doesn't mean that I know who, or what, God is. I don't. I don't really understand anything about God at all. That is the Rationalist agnostic viewpoint. I'm sorry. All I can say is: 'Give me proof.' Give me something to hold on to. Something I can believe in.

So I have no right to say to any Higher Divinity: "Why did you take Cain?" As it stands I can't, I have to be satisfied with the belief that it was a flaw of nature which caused the fatal worm to invade his body. That I was subject to a random act of chance and there was nothing I could do to change it.

Even so, if I look at the universe I see that it seems to be put together in a sensible manner. Designed by an architect, built by a competent carpenter. Almost like it was made by one of us. The greatest mystery of all. Let us leave it at that.

They were lonely years after Cain died. No, lonely is not the right word for there were the children, the friends, gardeners, Rationalists, committees, musicians. I was never alone. It would be impossible for me not to be surrounded by people. There was just an empty space where something should have been. After a year I thought I should find myself another man, but there was no-one there. No one there for me. Not someone that I wanted to be with. The children grew up, went their own ways... and then Father came to live with me. At threescore years and ten he had retired and settled down to write a book about the life and teaching of Jesus Christ. A continuation of his work in the church.

On Father's seventy-first birthday Robbie and his wife Molly were invited to my house to celebrate the occasion.

Of course Molly and her son, William, were visitors who came to see me yesterday. These days Molly is plump, satisfied, placid. Almost as old as me, she seems to want to go on for ever.

"We've both had happy lives," she said to me one day. "It comes from living with Christian men. There were times when I wondered, but it was happy in the end."

When she first met Robbie, Christ was nowhere near to entering her life. She was a good time girl. What we called a tart in those days. Dressed in red with a black ribbon at her throat. Well no, I never really met her at the time, but it's how I imagined it. She lived in a world that was alien to me, yet excited me with its decadence. The kind of person you would expect to attract the attentions of a confidence trickster. Then by some accident she became pregnant and bore her son, William. Our family weren't told officially about him until years later. She lived with Robbie off and on. Not long before he was ordained they married and, strangely, had a good life together. "Christ came into my heart," she said, although I did not believe it at the time.

Her son, William, was the only person not to be casually dressed. He has to wear a business suit when he goes visiting because he is the General Manager of a moderately large export/import company. Typical businessman you know, flash car, flash house, flash wife, flash overdraft, but he does have a flair for honesty which is quite out of the usual mould in the business world. He told me a little while ago that he wasn't going to make any of his staff redundant. Just a fad he said, you get rid of your experienced staff at great cost and before you know it they have to be replaced by new staff without the training. Making staff redundant is going out of fashion now I believe, but I'm sure the consultants and accountants will think of something else to replace it. How else can they remain in business?

Father had had a visitor, a member of his old congregation. When the visitor left he came into the kitchen in his cardigan and slippers. I had decided to cook a special meal for the birthday and was preparing the bird.

"A special roast for me is it?" he asked.

"I hoped it would be a surprise."

"You can't keep things secret from me. I'll make us a cup of tea."

He pottered around while I finished preparation. It was a duckling with orange and lemon stuffing. Eventually I had it in the oven on low heat. We sat at the table with cups of tea and a plate of biscuits..

"The nights are starting to draw in," he said.

"It's autumn Father." I'd spent the morning sweeping up the dead leaves and burning them in the incinerator. I'd tried to make compost of them once but they never broke down in a large mass. Furnace ashes give good potash.

"He had a lot to say for himself, that chap."

"He didn't tire you?"

"Goodness no. A new lease of life. I'll have a nap later. I love it when members of the old congregations drop in. Do you remember him?"

"Yes. And I remember his grandfather." This day came back to me. The Ugly Jesus day. I remembered the violin and what I learnt. The last spring of my childhood, before the bright colours, the flowers, the smells, the innocent joy in the world were tarnished by the departure from Eden.

"Ah yes, Old Daniels. You would have been a child..."

"He was very impressed by your famous sermon about Jesus being ugly."

"You remember that?"

"Quite clearly. Mrs. Robinson-Smythe gave you the cold shoulder."

"Strange you should remember... Now I seem to recall that Mrs. Robinson-Smythe had fundamentalist tendencies. How great a barrier to her understanding." Father looked at his fingernails abstractly, deep in thought. "Old Daniels told me later he thought my sermon was a revelation. Ever since then he made the family come along to my services. God bless his soul. If only a few more people like him had made their voices heard...."

"It was the day I learnt to play the violin properly."

"The violin? Really? Why would you learn the violin on such a day?"

"I practiced because I felt sorry for ugly Jesus."

"Oh dear." Father took a gingernut from the plate on the table and dunked it in his tea. "The report that he was ugly does not have a great deal of authority. Nowadays I think that he was probably quite handsome. That's the picture I have in my mind. At least his thoughts were handsome."

"His thoughts? Yes I suppose they were."

"You must believe that, even though you are a Rationalist."

My Rationalism was a heart I had worn on my sleeve all my life. I had shouted it out impetuously from the rooftops. It would have been better if I'd been quieter. Now I had to find the humility to admit to my father that these precious thoughts had changed. "I'm a Liberal Rationalist."

"Oh. What's a Liberal Rationalist?"

"A Rationalist that's liberal."

Father smiled and sipped his tea. "I should have known better than to ask you a simple question."

"A Radical Rationalist will say there's no truth in the New Testament whatsoever."

"Yes, that was Montague's position."

"That's what Montague said his position was."

"Oh?"

I remembered Montague in those last days, his face tombstone white, trying not to let me know of the pain. "You had convinced Montague that there was something to Christianity you know."

"Did I now? If only he had asked for Communion."

"He didn't want Communion. I think he wanted to study the ideas of Jesus because he thought he might learn something from them."

"Ah yes. The eternal pragmatist."

Montague had told me that he didn't believe in any afterlife. That he would just snuff out like a candle in a gust of wind, and all the doings of his life, all the journeys and discoveries, would resolve to a faint vapour which would quickly dissipate. "He didn't believe it was possible to commune with God."

"That's where we differ." Father stood up, walked around, took on his sermonising stance. "When Jesus was baptised by John in the River Jordan the Gospels say that a spirit descended upon him. He must have told his disciples about the experience. I think the voice from heaven was a later embellishment. What we have here is a symbol of the birth of his communion with God. That's the essential Christian experience. Not an academic study of ideas. Not a lot of wild and woolly theology."

But that was all that I could accept about his religion. A study of ideas. "You are talking about some sort of mystic experience?"

"Yes I suppose I am. A moment when God was revealed. I wanted to know whether such a revelation could be experienced by others."

"And you think it had?"

"It comes to very few. Paul on the way to Damascus. Brother John in his kitchen." He put his cup and saucer down on the table and walked about the room. "I had an experience when I was twenty. I went for a walk in the bush and came upon a stream flowing into a quiet pool, surrounded by a bank covered with moss and fern. Suddenly the whole of creation became still. Then I saw God, I felt God, in the water, in the trees, in everything. I had been in a church earlier that day and I knew that Jesus had led me to the revelation. I knew then that I would find God through Jesus. From that moment I was committed."

I opened the oven door, looked at the bird, basted it. A completely unnecessary action. My pragmatic mind you see. I can only accept what I can touch and feel. All this talk of communication with some abstract God up in heaven. It could just as well have been his imagination. Some momentary short-circuit in the brain. A passing fancy. But it was something he had often spoken of. "You mentioned that in one of your sermons."

"I did. You never had an experience like that?"

"No Father."

"Strange it should not come to everyone..."

"Few I would imagine."

"Very few have the call." He picked up the cup and saucer, leant against the mantelpiece. "In my early days I was very brash and impetuous. I'm sure I must have cut a very dashing figure. The young unmarried ladies in the congregation were always hovering around, but then I met your mother. That settled me down. I started to think about the meaning of the Gospels that had come down to us. I came to certain conclusions. I asked the congregation to question the articles of faith because I wanted them to see beyond the petty mores of convention. I believed the church had become a moribund establishment, but that it could be enlivened by the well of life which gushes forth from Christ. The living water he spoke of. There was opposition from many quarters in Church and congregation. Even in his own time Christ was disbelieved."

"It's the case with all new ideas Father."

"I had the same reservations about our Christian faith that you have. I remember the long discussions I had with Montague. I had to agree with much of what he said. He asked me to question my faith. I did. The difference was that I saw God in the crystal water."

"I think you were a better Rationalist then Montague ever was."

"I pride myself that I was."

"Well Father, I would call you a Christian Rationalist."

"Yes, perhaps I am. The church certainly needs rationality at times..."

He sat back down at the table and poured himself another cup of tea from the pot. He put in his usual spoon of sugar and stirred pensively. I accepted that Father would have these ideas about the reality of God and the experience of God. Was I being a wayward daughter by not having the same ideas? But no, I had never experienced a vision of God in the waters. There was no mystical experience I could believe in. Could I apologise for this?

"Did it worry you that I gave up Christianity?" I had to ask him.

"Yes."

"I'm sorry about that." It was a banal thing to say. I couldn't think of anything else. Then something that had worried me, that I had regretted. "Was I self indulgent?"

"Yes." He put his hand on mine. "You were."

"I'm sorry."

"You might be sorry, but you created a real crisis of faith. What was wrong if I could not show my own daughter the way to Christ. Especially since my son had gone astray. It was a dark time for me. I could say nothing, all I could do was hope."

"I didn't realise. I was very headstrong."

"You still are."

"You have to have the courage of your..." I couldn't say it. I just didn't know what to say. Of course I have a right to my own ideas. But the harm they do to others. Headstrong. Arrogant.

"Millicent forgave you."

"What do you mean?"

"On that final day. She was in my arms. In that final moment. The illness went. She said she was sorry for being such a silly girl and that when we all met again everything would be forgiven."

"Father! You don't mean to say that my going astray had any effect on Mother."

"She was telling me that it was the illness that let it affect her."

I remembered that when Mother began to get ill I was so arrogant. I felt that she should know how I thought. That it would teach her something.

"I'm sorry." It was all I could say.

"Don't be sorry. It is forgiven."

I took away my hand, went to the oven. No reason to go to the oven. I was afraid I might cry. But there were no tears. I fussed with the bird and came back to the table.

"That will be the most cared for duckling in Christendom," said Father.

"I never wanted to do anything to hurt Mother," I replied.

"I know. There's nothing to fret about now."

I wished I could believe him. All our lives we do things we fret about. We regret having done them. No amount of remorse can undo the results of a thoughtless act.

He put his hand back on mine. "I was concerned when you left the church, but you never left the teaching. That's a victory in a way. I was concerned about Robbie also. He had to follow a strange path to find God, and he did in the end."

I took away my hand away. Robbie the turd. Robbie who sold his soul to God for usury. Here was Father saying that it was the Christian ethic to forgive, yet I could not bring myself to do that. What was he doing as chaplain in a prison? Getting involved in crime with his old accomplices no doubt.

"You don't need to look at the oven again."

"No, Father."

"I don't know why you have this thing about Robbie. He is doing good work you know."

"It's something between him and me." I had nothing more to say.

"Whatever it is you must forgive."

"Oh don't preach to me. Don't preach."

"All right then. If you wish." He drained his cup and put it down.

"Now I must have my nap."

When Robbie and Molly arrived for the birthday dinner Molly was wearing a new fur coat. Father looked askance. "You have a rich patron my boy? A fur coat on a prison chaplain's stipend?"

"One of my flock put me onto a good thing," replied Robbie.

"Fell off a truck," I said.

"The good Lord provides for his own."

"The mills of God move in mysterious ways," said Molly, pleased to be in the comfort and prestige of a fur coat.

"It's a lovely coat," I said. "It suits you too." It did suit Molly who, naturally, had a regal air.

I remembered a conversation I once had with Robbie.

"God must have invented people like me for the ministry," he had said.

"What do you mean."

"When I was a crim I conned good people into believing that I was going to deliver some sort of benefit to them. Now I'm conning bad people into believing they're going to receive some reward in heaven."

"Well aren't they?"

"Well I don't know. How should I know. I've never met anyone who's been to heaven."

"The church teaches that there is a heaven Robbie. Didn't they tell you about that in seminary?"

"Oh they told me. They never gave me a train ticket to visit."

This was a conversation that disgusted me at the time because I believed that Robbie was betraying Father's principles. Whenever I had mentioned something like this to Father he merely said that God had given Robbie special training for His work. Saying something like that to me! A Rationalist!

Over dinner we discussed the children. Luke had left university and I wasn't sure what he was going to do with his life. Anne couldn't come because she was out on a date with her new boyfriend who was a Roman Catholic. That was Charles, of course, whom she eventually married. William had been appointed a junior executive in a large conglomerate. It appeared that none of the children were destined for the ministry.

Robbie proposed a toast for Father's good health and the success of his book. Father replied with a rambling speech. He felt he had a mission to change the direction of Christianity. "It must change or die." He felt that he had made a contribution but there was a great deal of work to be done yet. There was always resistance to change and a large body, like the church, was hard to move. A series of small pushes in the same direction would help achieve this. He hoped that his book might assist in a small way. He blessed us for being his family and supporting him.

Eventually the book was published. It caused a stir in its time and went into three impressions. Today it gathers dust on the library shelf.

"This has been a most enjoyable meal," said Father at last. We were sitting at table amongst the remnants of dessert, feeling that there should have been more than just two bottles of wine.

"I'd like to offer a vote of thanks," said Robbie holding up his empty glass. When I did not reply he continued. "I may have a posting to Auckland. There's a vacancy in the maximum security prison."

"A promotion Robbie?" I asked, thinking in my uncharitable way of his attachment to ambition.

"They've asked me if I'd take it on. Seems I do a satisfactory job here. All I need to do is get permission."

Molly smiled to herself. "If there's a calling... I'm sure we'll come back here one day."

Father went to his room and came back with a bottle of South African wine. "I was keeping it for Christmas. We have to drink to your success Robbie."

So the party continued on.

"I think God really meant for me to take on this job. All that past criminal offending was just training for a higher vocation," said Robbie.

"The mills of God move in mysterious ways," said Molly.

"It was meet that we should make merry, and be glad: for this thy brother was dead and is alive again; and was lost, and is found."

I said nothing.

After the wine Father offered to do the dishes, in spite of my protests. "You shouldn't have to do dishes after cooking a duckling like that," he said.

"I agree," said Molly. They collected the plates and glasses and went into the kitchen.

"Would you like a cigar?" Robbie took a slim packet of small round cigars from his pocket.

"You call those cheroots." I said.

"Same difference." I took one. He lit both his and mine. I never smoke, except for a cigar on certain special occasions. "Pipe of peace?"

"Hardly." I looked up at the ceiling and tried to blow smoke rings.

"Come on give us a break."

"Why should I?" I wasn't about to be affected by his false charm.

"You should forgive you know. The Father forgave the son and killed the fatted calf."

"I'm not anybody's father."

"Come on Sis, all that crime, it's in the past now."

"Yes, I know that."

"Then why won't you forgive me?"

"Because you never gave it up. What you're doing is just a con. You don't believe in Christianity. You never saw God in a pool of water."

"Did Matthew tell you about that?"

"Yes."

"No I didn't see that. I tell you Sis, I tell you truly, I took on this job because I needed it. I'm prepared to admit to that. Whether I believe in Christianity or not, it doesn't matter. I'm doing the right thing. I'm doing good. That's why they want me to go up to Auckland. Because I'm good at my job. Whether it's in the name of God or what. What more can the old fellow up there want from me?"

"I think he'd want someone who wasn't such a hypocrite."

"Ways and means. Ways and means. We are all Rationalists in this family, we should be able to see eye to eye."

"I don't want to talk about it." He was pandering. I hated it. We sat in silence. He took out his deck of cards.

"I can show you a trick with twenty-two cards."

"And tell me a story about an actress and a bishop."

"That too."

"Put them away."

He sighed and put his cards away. Then came the moment of truth. Kismet. The moment when all my sins were revealed.

"One of my flock has a message for you."

"What would I have in common with one of your flock?"

"You remember Jim Peabody?"

"You mean Jimmy Peabody?"

"Yes. James Williams Peabody. We used to call him Jimmy when we were kids."

"Well?"

"He confessed something to me. He asked me to tell you. He said he felt bad about it."

"I can't think of anything about Jimmy Peabody that might be of interest. What was it?"

"You remember those fancy dress dances we used to have? One time when you were playing the violin." This could not be true. This could not be true. "He said he did a turd in your violin case. He wanted me to apologise on his behalf."

I did not know what to say.

"I didn't know that anything like this ever happened Sis. I thought you would have made a fuss about it."

"I thought it was you."

"You thought it was me?"

"Yes."

"Why didn't you say?"

"How could one forgive a thing like that?"

"So you carried that crap around with you for the whole of your life?"

"Yes."

"No wonder I'm the Devil."

"Yes."

"Remember what the old chap said: 'Forgive us our trespasses…'"

It was then that I understood the Christian principle of forgiveness and how lack of it might sour your life.

So where does this leave me in the philosophical arena? I believe that I could be called a Christian Rationalist. No, I can't accept the mythology that surrounds the church, that Christ was the Son of God, that He died to save us from our sins, that His mother was a virgin. I can't even accept his conception that God was a Father, living in heaven, directly involved in human affairs. What I can accept is that his teaching of love, reconciliation and forgiveness is one of the most important innovations presented to mankind. Let's leave it at that and try to live up to the ideal.

11

It is morning at last. A light is creeping through the curtains at the window. I can hear distant sounds of the day awakening. The day staff are up and about their business.

My father died at the age of eighty after a long and honourable life. His funeral service was well attended. Loyal colleagues in the church, past members of his congregations and many admirers were present. In my garden I planted for him a rose of remembrance - the Rambling Rector. It is a vigorous vine and absolutely covers the trellis that Luke built for me with masses of fragrant white flowers. When I look at them they remind me of the rows of pure white faces sitting in the pews of his church, listening to his holy words.

Before Robbie went to Auckland I asked him for his forgiveness. He just smiled, took out his deck of cards and asked me if I knew the one card trick. That day he attempted to teach me fifty two card tricks, and I pretended to master them all. We sat at the table with Molly and a bottle of whisky. And exchanged ecclesiastical jokes.

Three nuns in a taxi....

Q. What did Eve say to Adam when she gave him the apple?
A. That's a hard one.

The old maid who died and lost her virginity when she was nailed in the coffin.

What the bishop really said to the actress.

I blush to tell you these stories, but then I've heard a few in the course of my life. Robbie died after living exactly three score years and ten. I planted a striking rose for him. Old Black, because he was the black sheep of the family, who finally made good. It's name in the catalogues is 'Nuits de Young'. The flowers are small doubles, not black but deep maroon-purple with a bright gold centre. And very fragrant. I like the purple. It reminds me of the colour of a bishop's shirt. I'm sure that Robbie is a bishop in heaven. Or maybe he went down below, because that was where his flock was.

I know it is the last day. These are just pictures taken at random from the dream of my life. Moments of pain, happiness, times you were sorry about something you did. They're held in my memory now but where do they go when I die? Just vanish into the blue horizon I suppose. Or do I carry them with me, vague impressions, into another life?

But what do these images mean? String them together to form a story and what do you have? The Rake's Progress? The problems encountered when you have strong religious beliefs? How we care for the people we love?

No, the Christian religion is not the centre of this story nor are my beliefs. It is the people in my life that are important, and how I got on with those that I loved. It's what I did and how I did it that counts. It doesn't matter what we believe, or what we have done, we all have to face this moment in time, this discarding of the carnate flesh. All we can hope is that we have not exactly wasted our time here on earth. That things might perhaps be a little better for our having been here. I cannot ask for any reward other than my own happiness. Now people like Hitler, what can they take with them... And then the fundamentalist Christian who fondly believes that the gates of heaven will open... What will they find when they pass over the river?

I have no theories concerning the meaning of life. Our greatest poet found it to be of no significance, a tale told by an idiot, and so did Sad Sam Beckett. But life was worth living. It was an experience of some moment, sometimes happy, sometimes sad; and you did learn something. I would never be so pessimistic to say that life was worth nothing. I might be forgotten in a hundred years, but still there is a small voice crying in the wind, a ripple which never dies in the ocean of time. You find love, amusement, good friends, what more could you want?

I'm the last person left of my generation. The last person in the family. They all went one way or another. But I feel they are very close somehow, close enough for someone to want to come and talk to me.

There's a vision there. In my mind a hallucination. It's Robbie, Robbie in his bishop's cloth. How are you Robbie? Talk to me.

"I'm fine Lucy, I'm fine."

And you are enjoying heaven are you?

"I don't know. The Old Man's started to let Catholics in."

The same old Robbie.

"And it was me that put the frog in the baptismal font. I have to admit it after all these years."

Ah, honesty at last. Don't go, don't go. Ah the ghosts from the past haunt my dreams.

And there is Cain, standing there waiting for me. And Montague with him. I am sure Montague would have been very disappointed to have ended up in heaven. What does he tell me?

"We'll have to discuss this philosophy in greater detail my dear."

Of course we will. Of course. And Cain, do you have something to say?

"There is a marked difference of opinion on certain subjects."

The afterlife will not be boring it appears.

And Mother and Father, together, and so young again, holding hands. Mother you pick flowers, Iceland poppies, and caress them in your arms like you would a baby. Mother... Those are your flowers and you have picked them. As you sow, so shall you reap... Give those flowers to your little girl Mother.

Hello little girl, what's your name?

"Lucinda. You can call me Lucy if you like."

Don't I know you?

"A long time ago."

Ah yes, a long time ago. Do you know Robbie?

"I have a little brother called Robbie. He's naughty, he puts frogs in the baptismal font. But I'm going to forgive him. You have to forgive those who trespass against you."

Indeed. May I have those flowers you are holding in your arms?

"Here you are. I've been in Mother's garden and picked them."

These are nice flowers. I always said I'd take flowers with me when I went.

"Here. Are you going away on a train ride?"

Something like that. An expected journey.

"In that case I'll wave good-bye to you."

Good-bye.

I was dreaming? No, here are the flowers. I think things are clear at last. I told my daughter that she had to plant a rose for me, and tend the other roses in my garden of remembrance. She'll remember her grandmother and her grandfather like she always does. And her father. And her uncle.

Look it's dawn, I've been awake all night. Maybe it's time to sleep at last. And take these flowers to the world that owns them. When I was a young woman I saw the dragonfly above a pool of still water and wondered about the frailty of life and whether there was a light of eternity at the end. I don't know what is there. An Almighty God with clouds of angels singing - or just darkness - just the night. I'll take my chances. It's not what you believe, it's what you are that counts.

Montague, Mother, Father, Robbie, Cain, that little girl I once was, I'm coming now. I'll bring you flowers. This old life, it's been so funny and sad, a world of light and shadow. In the end all our petty affairs dissolve into dust. Nothing is ever perfect. Nothing is ever finished. But I'm not going to argue any more, I'll just wave goodbye to it all.

Recent and forthcoming titles from ESAW

Tiger Words
Paekakariki Poets $10

Music Therapy
Peter Olds (poetry) $15

the smell of oranges
Jill Chan (poetry) $15

Dumber
Mark Pirie (poetry) $15

The Singing Harp
Iain Sharp (poetry) $15

The Road Goes On
Brian E. Turner (novel) $35

Travel and other compulsions
Heather McPherson (poetry) $18

To . . .
Bill Dacker (poetry) $15

Bookmarks
Winter Readings at Arty Bees Bookshop $15

They Drank Kava
Moshé Liba (poetry) $15

The Estuary of Komo
Moshé Liba (poetry) $15

take a seat and rest awhile
Rosalind Derby (artwork and text) $25

What Colours a Pākehā
Patrick Coogan (poetry and stories) $25

Also available:

Toku Tinihanga: *Selected Poems 1982 to 2002*
By Michael O'Leary: Published by **HeadworX** $20

Plus:

Toku Tinihanga a CD featuring Michael O'Leary with music by Trevor
Bycroft and Blackthorn. Recorded at Waimea Studios, Christchurch, for
ESAW (Sounds Division) $20

Greatest Hits Anthology of writing from **ESAW** and **HeadworX**
publishers. $30